Beatrice

Rescue Me Mail-Order Brides

Cheryl Wright

Beatrice
(Rescue Me Mail-Order Brides)

*Note: Beatrice is part of a multi-author series

Copyright ©2023 by Cheryl Wright

Cover Artist: Black Widow Books

Dedication

To Margaret Tanner, my very dear friend and fellow author, for her enduring encouragement and friendship.

To Alan, my husband of over forty-eight years, who has been a relentless supporter of my writing and dreams for many years.

To Virginia McKevitt, cover artist and friend, who always creates the most amazing covers for my books.

To You, my wonderful readers, who encourage me to continue writing these stories. It is such a joy knowing so many of you enjoy reading my stories as much as I love writing them for you.

Table of Contents

Chapter One

Crimson Point, Montana - 1884

Beatrice Gaffney glanced about before she stepped off the train. After all this time, she prayed she was safe.

She'd changed trains three times, waiting overnight in some towns, simply to ensure the trail went cold. Her trail. Until now, Beatrice did not know what it felt like to be wanted by the law. Well, that was a bit of an overreach. She wasn't wanted exactly, but she was certain she was being pursued. Unless she could change her identity, they would hound her until the day she died.

It was the very reason she gave in and became a mail-order bride. Only now she wasn't convinced it was the right thing to do. For one thing, she didn't know her groom. Second, just because she married and changed her name did not mean the people chasing her would stop looking for her.

It wasn't her fault, despite what she was certain everyone would be saying. Horace had tried to… she didn't even want to think about it. She had to defend herself, but how was she to know the outcome?

She shuddered at the memory. She'd high-tailed it out of there and hurried to see her best friend. Meg agreed the only option was for Beatrice to leave town. After all, she hadn't meant to do it. He might have been vulgar and disgusting, but he didn't deserve what she did to him.

She hurried home and packed a few essentials, then headed to the railway station. And now here she was, standing on the platform of the Crimson Point railway station. She was about to endure a hasty marriage to a man she did not know.

The memory of that fateful day still haunted her, and Beatrice was convinced it would for the rest of her days. Horace Thatcher was the most revolting man she'd ever met. He had groped at her one too many times, and the last time, she was determined not to let it continue. Except this time she killed him.

The station wasn't as busy as Beatrice had envisioned. Did that mean Crimson Point was a tiny backwater? She hoped not. What she really wanted was somewhere to blend in. Not a place where everyone knew each other.

Beatrice liked the busyness of where she'd come from. What she hadn't liked about Helena was Horace. He was supposed to be a co-worker, but instead, he harassed her every moment she was at work until it became unbearable.

"Excuse me. Are you Beatrice Gaffney?" The stranger stood a good foot taller than her, forcing her to lift her head way back to see him properly. Beatrice swallowed. Was she going from one difficult situation to another? She honestly didn't know. How could she?

She closed her eyes briefly, trying to decide if she needed to flee yet another man. "Miss? Miss Gaffney?" He frowned. "You've gone deathly white." He guided her to a wooden bench close to where they stood.

Beatrice sighed as she sat and swallowed again. "I am Beatrice," she said, her voice barely above a whisper. "You must be Mr. Harris?" She extended her hand, and he reached out to take it. Beatrice expected him to be rough, but he was gentle. He covered her small hand with both of his large ones, then sat down beside her.

"I am," he said. "Tyler Harris." He pulled his hat off his head then. "You appear unwell. We should visit the doctor. His rooms are just…"

"I'm fine," she blurted out, far more forcefully than intended. "It's the travel. I've spent…" she was about to say over a week, but that wouldn't ring true for him. "days on a train. I started my journey on a stagecoach, then had to change."

He nodded his understanding. "Well, you're here now, and I'm very pleased you are." He glanced about. "Is this all your luggage? Or do the porters have the rest?" He seemed curious more than anything, but Beatrice didn't have time to take too many of her belongings. The law would be on her trail. She was already certain she'd been followed. At least part of the way. When she suddenly left the train for the stagecoach back in Land's End, her pursuer didn't seem to notice. Poor fellow was probably still on the train believing she was there too.

"That's it. I didn't have a lot to bring." She didn't add she'd needed to flee at breakneck speed. He looked her up and down. Her gown was well-made and of good quality. Making her own gowns saved a substantial amount of money and allowed her to always look her best. "I have a little money," she said, keeping her voice low. "I plan to make more clothes when I am settled."

"Very well," he said, not sounding at all surprised. "Do you feel up to going straight to the church? Please tell me if you'd rather not."

He did not sound like a person who would be violent, and she thanked her lucky stars for that. "It really is fine. Provided you feel I am presentable."

He smiled, then looked her up and down. "You're beautiful. If you look like this after days of travel, I can't wait to see what you will be like once you're rested." Beatrice felt heat travel up her face. "You're even more pretty when you blush," he said as he chuckled. "Come on, let's go." He leaned down and picked up her bag, then carried it to the buckboard he had waiting outside. Her groom-to-be stored her belongings, then helped her up.

"Thank you," she said. She was shaking and wasn't sure what she could do about it.

"Are you sure this is what you want?" he asked. "You're trembling. I don't want you to feel forced into this."

Was she sure? Beatrice really wasn't certain. But she had to go through with it. "I'm certain. I haven't eaten for a bit, so perhaps that's why I'm shaking."

He frowned. "Then we shall visit the diner first, then go to the church." Tyler Harris seemed like a man who cared. She hoped he didn't turn out to be like Horace after all.

Beatrice had to hold back or she would have appeared like a greedy cowboy. She hadn't eaten a decent meal in days. A sandwich here and there, and pieces of fruit had been quick and easy to grab between stations. The stagecoach had afforded a little more time, but that was days ago.

She felt his eyes on her and glanced up to see him staring. A quick visit to a matrimonial agency secured this arrangement. They'd not had time to exchange letters, so all she knew was he was a rancher. She couldn't believe she was about to marry a man who worked the land. Beatrice had no experience with his occupation as she was brought up in town. She'd lived in one of the busiest towns in Montana and had worked in her mother's seamstress store for as long as she could remember. Until it burned to the ground with her mother inside.

The memory cut her to the core. Beatrice almost choked on her tea. "What can I do?" he asked gently. He looked stricken.

She finally got herself under control. "The tea went down the wrong way," she said, her voice a little scratchy. He probably thought the tears that danced on her eyelashes were because she'd choked. They weren't. Losing her mother in such a ghastly way was like having her heart ripped out of her chest.

It was then she had to seek outside employment. As luck would have it, there was an opening at the busy mercantile. It sat in the center of Helena and accommodated a huge number of travelers. They had customers from opening to closing time, and the shelves were being replenished several times a day. That necessitated her going into the storeroom frequently. Even on checking Horace wasn't there before she ventured in, he seemed to appear out of nowhere. Within minutes, he was groping her.

"Miss Gaffney? Beatrice? Are you alright?" Tyler Harris's voice seemed as though it came from an echo chamber, and she tried to focus.

She put her hands to her temple. "I have a bit of a headache. From the travel, I'm sure." Perhaps it was the relief of knowing she'd escaped. Got away with murder. Is that what she'd done? Her head pounded now, and all Beatrice wanted to do was lay down and sleep it off. She wasn't certain she could ever sleep away the knowledge she'd killed another person. Even if that person was pure evil.

Chapter Two

The marriage ceremony took less than twenty minutes, and that included the signing of the register. Tyler had hoped it would be a little longer, for the sake of his bride. Every woman wants the perfect wedding, but theirs was over and done with so quick, it almost felt like it didn't happen.

He had the marriage certificate in his pocket to prove it had.

Glancing across at his wife, she still appeared pale. Despite insisting she visit the doctor, she'd refused. He couldn't do more than that. She wanted to buy some material and other necessary supplies at the mercantile. It was the least he could do. She balked when he insisted on paying. He wondered if she didn't want to depend on him this early in their marriage.

Whatever the reason, he was certain there was something very wrong. What it was, he couldn't put his finger on, but Tyler was determined to find out. She was as jumpy as a rabbit. It was not how he expected his wife to be. He'd envisioned a carefree woman who would spend her time taking care of the house, cooking, and bearing children.

The way she acted now, he wasn't convinced she would even allow him to touch her. "We're almost there," he said, and she jumped. His voice had startled her out of wherever she had gone. Beatrice was silent for most of the one-hour trip home from Crimson Point. He'd hoped to use that time for them to get to know each other, even a little. "That's the archway to my property up ahead. Mountain High Ranch."

She sighed, and Tyler was certain it was with relief. She'd done so much traveling lately, she'd probably had enough.

"How many did you say there would be for supper?" She turned to him as she spoke. They were the most words she'd uttered since they'd left town.

"Seven, including us." He frowned then. "Did I mention my elderly mother lives here, too?"

Her expression was blank momentarily, then a brief smile crossed her lips. "No, you didn't. But it makes no difference. It will be nice having another woman to talk to."

He'd told her in town she'd have the extras to cook for. He'd even let her buy whatever groceries and other supplies she wanted. She would cook for the cowhands and his mother, so letting her choose meant the meals should be good. *Should.* He didn't know what sort of cook she was, and to be truthful, he probably should have asked. He'd just assumed.

She stared at the ranch house, not saying a word. He did not know if she was happy, disappointed, or overwhelmed. It was clear to Tyler this wouldn't be an easy marriage. He'd expected his wife to be happy and carefree. Beatrice was far from that.

His only hope was his mother could bring Beatrice out of her shell. She was good at putting people at ease. He continued down the drive and stopped outside the front door. "We're here," he said, then realized how silly that sounded.

He climbed down from the buckboard, then helped Beatrice down. She stared into his face as he lifted her to the ground, but he could see no interest there. Was it always going to be like this? He couldn't bear if it was. His only saving grace was her travel. It was clear Beatrice was exhausted. He couldn't even imagine traveling for days on end. He wearied at the trip into town and back, and that was only around an hour each way.

He glanced up to see his mother standing on the porch. She'd been so excited when he announced he'd sent for a mail-order bride. Living so far out of Crimson Point meant little opportunity for Tyler to socialize. He rarely went to the church dances and spent so little time in town he knew few people apart from the churchgoers. Even then, he didn't know several of them all that well.

Mother stepped forward, her hands outstretched. "Mother, this is Beatrice." Before his wife knew what was happening, she was wrapped in his mother's arms.

"Welcome, my dear. Welcome!" Tears flooded Maisy Harris's eyes. "I've waited so long for this." She put an arm around Beatrice's waist. "Come on inside and sit down. You must be exhausted."

"I am exhausted," Beatrice answered.

"I knew you would be. The kettle is about to boil. Tea or coffee?"

Tyler stood in the doorway, listening to the two women. They seemed to get on well. It meant he didn't have to worry about those two, only about his own relationship with his new wife. Of course, their marriage was a unique situation. They were strangers thrown together by a matrimonial agency. Neither had knowledge of the other, and they were starting from scratch.

Mother might be the one to break the barrier between them, but he couldn't rely on that. He carried Beatrice's luggage into their bedroom and placed it just inside the door. What she'd think about that, he wasn't certain, but his mother's advice was to start as he intended to continue. And that's exactly what he'd done.

This was his childhood home. Until his father had passed, this room had been his parents'. Little more than a year later, Mother announced she was moving into one of the spare rooms, and he was to take over the main bedroom and get himself a wife. He needed heirs to continue the family name.

Most families had at least six children, many had twelve. Mother had almost died birthing Tyler and could not conceive again after his birth. That meant he was the one and only chance of the family name continuing. He only hoped Beatrice could conceive. If she couldn't, he wasn't sure what he would do.

Tyler shook himself mentally. What was he even thinking? They'd barely spoken a word between them, and he was thinking about… that? He should be ashamed of himself. Tyler wasn't sure how he would face Beatrice after having such thoughts. If his mother knew, she would not be pleased.

"Your bags are in our bedroom," he announced as he walked through the combined kitchen and sitting room. "I'll fetch the groceries."

He was about to leave when his mother spoke. "I've made you a coffee, so don't be long." Tyler nodded, then continued outside. The last thing he needed was for a fox to get into their supplies.

They'd bought enough to last a few weeks at least, so there was quite a lot to bring in. "Hey, Boss,"

Earl, his foreman, said. "Need a hand?" He had jumped the fence before waiting for an answer.

"That would be wonderful," Tyler said. That coffee was calling out to him. The pair loaded up their arms and went inside.

"Coffee, Earl?" Maisy asked, but didn't wait for an answer. Earl removed his hat and placed it on the hat stand at the front door.

"Thank you, Ma'am," he said. "Once I'm done bringin' in the supplies." Maisy smiled. Tyler knew Earl was her favorite. He was always polite and amenable and would do anything to help.

"There's cake too," she said. Tyler watched his face light up. Earl loved his food, like every other cowboy on the property.

"We won't be much longer, Mother," Tyler called. "We're almost done."

"My goodness," he heard Maisy say as he left the house. "You must have just about bought out the store!"

That made him chuckle. Since she did the cooking, his mother knew exactly how much food was required to feed them all for three to four weeks.

With the groceries sitting on the countertop, they all sat around the table. Tyler could see both Beatrice and his mother were champing at the bit to put them away, but he put them off.

"Welcome, Mrs. Harris," Earl said when they were introduced. "You should like it here. Everyone is friendly. If you need anything, let me know. I'm always happy to help."

"Earl is my foreman," Tyler explained. "You'll meet the other hands later."

Beatrice had little to say, but that wasn't unexpected. She had spoken less than a few dozen words since they met. He couldn't stand constant chatter, but neither did he want to be living in near silence. How would he even know what she liked and didn't like if she didn't tell him?

Tyler was already regretting the marriage, but could tell Maisy adored her. "Beatrice bought fabric and supplies to make some gowns," he said, trying to bring Beatrice out of her self-imposed silence.

"You sew! How wonderful," Maisy exclaimed, her excitement clear.

Beatrice went quiet, more quiet than usual, and glanced down at the table. "My mother was a seamstress. I worked in the store with her." Her voice broke on the last words, and Tyler wondered about the story behind that.

"I'm sorry, my dear," Maisy said. "When did you lose her?" Tyler's head shot up. Beatrice hadn't mentioned her mother had died.

"A… a little over six months ago. There was a fire in the store, and…" Her voice did break then, and she turned away. Maisy ushered the men out of the room, and they hurried away. The last thing Tyler wanted to deal with was a crying woman. Today had been hard enough without tears as well.

Earl glanced at him as they snatched up their hats and hurriedly left the house.

Chapter Three

"I haven't used this old sewing machine in ages," Maisy said, as she uncovered it. "The fabric you chose is beautiful. The color will look lovely on you." She held the material up against Beatrice and smiled. "It suits your hazel eyes perfectly. I can't wait to see what you make with it."

Beatrice really liked Maisy. She was a lovely soul and seemed to understand Beatrice. Of course, she didn't know about the dreadful act she'd carried out, and Beatrice could never tell her. It was difficult living with such a devastating secret, but she had no choice. She was convinced if Tyler knew, he would turn her over to the law. It was something she dreaded, but knew she would eventually have to face the consequences of her actions.

To run the way she had was unforgiveable, especially given the fact she was certain the man was dead, but Horace had been unrelenting. He had no scruples and didn't care one iota about compromising her. Groping her had become a game to him, but this time he'd pushed the limit. He pushed her into a corner and grabbed her crotch.

He'd covered her mouth with his hand so she couldn't scream.

There was no doubt in Beatrice's mind what Horace had intended, and she shoved him away. After hitting his head on the way down, he lay lifeless on the floor.

"Are you alright, Beatrice? You've gone deathly pale." Maisy put a hand to Beatrice's shoulder, startling her. "Perhaps we should leave this to another day. I think a nap is in order."

Beatrice stared up at her. Maisy's concern was touching, and she already knew the pair were going to be friends. They'd only known each other for a matter of hours, but it felt as though they'd been acquainted for several years. Standing, Beatrice nodded. "There's plenty of time," she said as they left the spare room. A room she was certain was earmarked as a nursery for the future.

Maisy likely longed for grandchildren. Beatrice couldn't blame her. The woman was getting on in years. She certainly wasn't decrepit, but she wasn't young either.

"Let me show you around," Maisy said as she walked through the house, pointing out various rooms. "And this," she said with a flourish, "is where you and Tyler sleep." Beatrice swallowed hard. It had to eventually get to this point. "After your nap, you could put your clothes away." She opened the closet. "Tyler has cleared a hanging space for you, and this drawer is yours as well," she said, opening one drawer to the dresser. The mirror was a little tarnished, but was usable.

"Thank you, Maisy," she said. "You've made me feel at ease on a difficult day." Her mother-in-law pulled her close and hugged Beatrice. Then, without another word, left her alone.

She emptied the overnight bag that contained her small amount of clothing into the wardrobe and dresser drawer, then placed her hairbrush and other accessories on top. The realization of how little she now possessed hit Beatrice like a rock to the head. If only she'd had more time to collect her belongings.

The truth was, she didn't. Had she stayed around, Beatrice was certain she would have been arrested for murder. Oh, the shame of it all. Surely, being so far from where it all happened meant she wouldn't be found. She'd lost sight of the man who'd followed her on the train. Hopefully, that meant he had no clue where she was.

Could she breathe a sigh of relief, even if it was only for now? She certainly wouldn't count on it.

"Quiet," she heard Maisy whisper loudly. "Your wife needs to rest. The poor girl is exhausted."

Beatrice did not know how long she'd been asleep, but the room was in semi-darkness, so it had to be several hours. She slowly sat up, then headed toward the kitchen, but heard muffled voices. Were they talking about her? Since the voices were low, she would never know.

She heard a door slam, and then another. Did that mean…? She suddenly stood. It must be supper time, which meant Maisy had done what Beatrice had been brought here to do – cook. She felt sick to her stomach to think the elderly woman had taken over her job out of necessity.

She hurried into the kitchen. "I'm so sorry, Maisy," she said, taking a pot of stew from Maisy's hands. "I can't believe I slept for so long." She placed the dish in the center of the table, then reached for the freshly baked loaf of bread. When she glanced up, Tyler was staring at her, a smile on his face.

What are you staring at? she wanted to ask, but didn't dare. Her first day in her new home, and she didn't want to push her luck. She'd already burst into tears once and had no intention of upsetting herself again. If she kept it up, her husband was sure to send her back home, and that would never do.

No doubt she would walk right into the arms of the law. She would be locked up and eventually hanged. That's what they did to murderers, no exceptions.

Even if it was out of self-defense, she was certain that would not be an adequate excuse.

"Did you sleep well?" Tyler asked as he continued to stare. He stood then and came over to her, his hand moving to her cheek. He leaned in close, and Beatrice was convinced he was about to kiss her. "Your hair is over your face," he whispered. "You might want to fix it," he said, then went back to his place at the head of the table.

Beatrice let go of the breath she didn't know she was holding. Would it really be so bad if he kissed her? There would surely be a time when he did for real. He was her husband, after all. She was certain it wouldn't stop there, and she was truly terrified of what might happen then. Would he be as rough with her as Horace had been, or would Tyler be gentle and caring?

She felt sure Tyler was the caring kind, and that made her feel reassured about the inevitable marital relations that would surely result from this marriage.

"Beatrice? Where did you go?" Maisy's motherly voice cut through her musings and Beatrice glanced about. The four cowhands were seated around the large table, along with Tyler. Maisy stood by her side, her hand on Beatrice's shoulder. "It's fine," she whispered. "I know you're exhausted."

"You sit here next to me," Tyler said, a grin on his face. The moment the women sat, he introduced everyone. "You already know Earl, my foreman. This is Clyde, Buster, and Duke," he said, pointing to each one. "My wife, Beatrice."

Each man greeted and welcomed her, making Beatrice feel more at home. "Now for grace," Maisy said. Each person bowed their heads and Maisy said a simple but heartwarming prayer. "Thank you, Lord, for the food on our table, and for those we share it with. We are also grateful for Beatrice, who now shares our table and our lives. Amen."

Warmth filled Beatrice. She was so grateful to have Maisy. The woman was a godsend, and had already proven herself to be a friend to her new daughter-in-law. Beatrice's mother would have adored her, and they would have got on well.

Determined not to fall into a blubbering mess again, Beatrice lifted her fork. Tyler leaned in and whispered in her ear. "Are you alright?" His words surprised her because he didn't seem to care much earlier. He had been more than a little indifferent, not worried about her at all. Still, she couldn't blame him. She was a complete stranger to him, just as he was to her.

And tonight she was expected to give herself to that stranger. The thought made her shudder, but at least he was kind. Unlike Horace. She closed her eyes and shook her head. Beatrice wasn't sure she could do this.

She suddenly stood and shoved back her chair. She ran outside, slamming the door behind her.

The front door opened, and Beatrice sensed it was Maisy before she turned to see who was there. "I'm sorry," she said quietly. "I don't know what came over me."

Maisy sat down next to her and put an arm around Beatrice's shoulder. "You're in a new place, with a bunch of complete strangers." Her arm went up, and she rubbed her hand over her daughter-in-law's back. "You are likely overwhelmed."

"Tyler is probably furious."

Maisy chuckled. "He has no idea what he is doing. Give him time. Give yourself time. Get to know each other better, understand how the other thinks."

Beatrice turned and studied the other woman. "I'm not the person you think I am," she whispered.

"My dear girl," Maisy said firmly. "I know nothing about you except you seem quite vulnerable." She reached across and held Beatrice's hand. "We're family now. I don't need to know about your past, only your future. We've all had indiscretions in our past. It doesn't mean we have to air our dirty laundry for all and sundry." She smiled tentatively. "Some things are best kept to ourselves."

She so badly wanted to tell Maisy, but if she did, the woman would surely tell the local sheriff. Instead, Beatrice bit her tongue. Whether she could live with her *indiscretion* was another thing entirely.

Maisy suddenly stood. "Time to go back inside. Our food is getting cold, and the men will crave dessert soon." She laughed then. "There are two things men want – one is food. The other we won't talk about." She pulled her lips into a tight line.

Beatrice didn't want to talk about it either, but knew she was dreading it.

With the dishes washed and dried and the kitchen cleaned up, the two women joined Tyler by the fireside. He motioned for her to join him, then pulled Beatrice onto his knee. "Tell me about yourself," he said, then slid an arm around her middle.

"There's little to tell," she said. "I'm a seamstress. At least I was until the store burned down."

Tyler frowned. "You didn't rebuild the store?"

It was the last thing Beatrice wanted to talk about, but the more she did, the easier it would become. At least she thought it would. "I couldn't bring myself to do it. I received a small sum from the insurance company and moved on."

"And then you came here?"

He was asking a lot of questions, and it bothered Beatrice. "Then I worked at the mercantile for a short time before I came here." *Until I killed a man.*

"I see," he said, but he really didn't.

"Tyler," Maisy said sharply. "Leave the girl alone. She's had a long few days and needs to rest." She looked thoroughly annoyed, and Beatrice appreciated her intervention.

He studied Beatrice then. "I apologize. Mother is right. You look tired. We have an early start here on the ranch, so we should retire for the night."

Beatrice swallowed. The moment she'd been dreading had finally arrived. Her only hope was Tyler was gentle with her. She stood, and he took her hand, then led her to their bedroom.

Chapter Four

Beatrice awoke to the rising sun. Tyler was stirring next to her.

"Good morning," he said, a grin on his face. He leaned over and lightly kissed her lips. Last night hadn't been as bad as she'd envisioned, and now she was Tyler's wife in every sense of the word.

"Good morning," she said. Beatrice managed a smile, and it seemed to make her husband happy. "I need to make breakfast," she told him, climbing out of the bed. Tyler had other ideas and snaked his arm around her waist, pulling her back into the bed. Was this what married life was going to be like? With her husband demanding his husbandly rights and her having no choice in the matter?

He would surely tire of it once the novelty wore off. Today she would give into him, but once she had a routine, he would need to understand she had things to do.

There was a light tap at the door. Beatrice sighed with relief. "Come in," she called, believing Maisy to be on the other side.

"Good morning," Maisy said, a huge smile on her face. "How did you sleep? Do you feel up to helping with breakfast?"

"Of course," Beatrice said. "But I'm the one who is supposed to do most of the cooking, not you." She climbed out of bed and pulled her robe around herself. As she glanced back, Tyler's disappointment was obvious. Beatrice almost chuckled out loud, but held back.

Once in the kitchen, Maisy pottered about, pulling pans out of the cupboard, filling the kettle, and placing cups on the countertop. "What would you like me to do?" she asked Maisy. She felt useless watching the older woman. She was obviously well-versed in the running of the ranch kitchen.

"You can prepare the cups for coffee. It won't be long and the men will be here. We need the plates out of the cupboard. Oh, and you can set the table."

Maisy began frying sausages, and had a plate with eggs sitting beside the stove, ready to cook. "You've already collected the eggs," Beatrice said, disappointed she couldn't undertake that menial task.

"These are left over from yesterday. I'll take you out later and show you the hiding places our chickens have." She chuckled then, and warmth filled Beatrice. Maisy was like her mother in a lot of ways. They would have been about the same age, too.

How she missed her mother, but Beatrice knew she needed to look to the future, rather than the past. "I'll need the bacon from the icebox," she added as she turned the sausages.

Beatrice took it all in. Tomorrow she would be up early enough to undertake what was now her job. Maisy deserved a sleep in.

"Run along and get dressed, Beatrice. The men will be here soon."

Beatrice glanced down at herself. She was still in her nightgown and robe, and that would never do. She felt so at home here; she hadn't even thought about the fact she wasn't dressed. By the time she returned, everyone was sitting at the table except Maisy. Beatrice poured the coffee and placed one in front of each man. Soon, their breakfast was ready.

After grace was said, everyone tucked into their food. These were hardworking men, and they needed a big breakfast. From today onward, Beatrice vowed to ensure they got the best start to the day she could give them. Maisy had born the burden for far too long. She'd promised to teach Beatrice the ropes, and that was fine, but the moment she was able, Beatrice would take over and give the older woman the break she deserved.

"More coffee?" Maisy was on her feet before Beatrice even knew what was going on. She refilled each of the men's cups, then began to clear the dishes away.

"You rest," Beatrice said. "I can do that." Tyler smiled at her, and it sent shivers down her spine.

He drained the rest of his cup, then stood. "I'm off," he said, then leaned over and kissed her cheek. "See you at lunch."

"Thanks for breakfast," Earl said as he stood, and the other cowhands mimicked his words.

They all stood then, and the five men headed for the front door, grabbing their hats on the way.

Silence overtook the room as they all left, and Beatrice savored it. She'd never lived on a ranch, and this was all very new to her.

"Quiet, isn't it?" Maisy asked as she chuckled. She reached over and patted Beatrice's hand. "You'll get used to it. Now, it's time for *us* to sit and rest, then the real work begins." She refilled both their cups with tea, and led Beatrice outside. "I love this time of day. Watching the sun rise brings its own kind of peace."

Beatrice followed her gaze and had to agree. It was a beautiful time of day. No wonder Maisy liked to sit and enjoy it each morning. With the birds singing all around them, and the low murmurs of the animals waking up for the day, she'd heard nothing better.

It wasn't like this in town, far from it, and Beatrice decided she liked it out here.

Maisy suddenly reached over and took her hand. "I'm glad you married my son. I hope you have a long and happy life with him." She wiped at her eyes, then suddenly stood. "Time for us to prepare for the day." Without further ado, Maisy snatched up both their cups and hurried inside.

When the men arrived for lunch, the bread was still warm. The thick vegetable soup was cooked to perfection, and blueberry muffins stood cooling on the countertop. The apple pie would be ready by the time it was needed. When the pie came out, the lamb would take its place, Maisy told her. Later, they would add the vegetables for roasting, but not this early in the day.

Maisy ran her kitchen like a well-oiled machine, and Beatrice needed to learn to do the same.

She thought it would be an effortless task to take over from Maisy, but she could see now it wouldn't be. Her mother-in-law had a routine, one she'd carried out for many years. How Beatrice thought she could walk in and learn it all in one day she would never know.

"More soup, Clyde?" Maisy asked, and he nodded. Beatrice helped dish out a second bowl for all the men. Tyler said little at lunch. Instead, he studied her. Had she done something wrong, or was he merely curious about her? Beatrice would probably never know.

Tyler handed her his bowl and Beatrice refilled it, then cut additional slices of bread for the men. It exhausted her thinking about all the cooking they'd done that morning, let alone the chores they still had to do. She was ready for a long nap, but it was the last thing either woman had time for.

Not that she could say it out loud, but Beatrice was exhausted. First, it was the extended travel she'd done, and now it was from non-stop cooking and looking after the men. Had she made the second biggest mistake of her life? The first was accepting a position at the mercantile where Horace worked. In both cases, it was too late to turn back.

A hand to her shoulder brought Beatrice back to the present. "Are you alright, dear?" Maisy asked, concern written all over her face.

Beatrice forced a smile, although the last thing she felt right now was happiness. "I'm just tired." She shrugged her shoulders. "I'm not used to this sort of work."

Maisy leaned in close. "You'll get used to it, I promise. Soon you'll forget you ever felt this way."

Nodding, Beatrice continued to refill the bowls for the men, then pulled the apple pie out of the oven and sliced it, then served it into the bowls that sat waiting to be filled. The clotted cream was already in a bowl on the countertop.

"Come and sit here with me," Tyler said, patting the chair she'd occupied earlier. "You look ready to drop."

She glanced across at Maisy, who nodded. How long would it take for her to get used to this fast pace of running a ranch kitchen? They were only halfway through the day, and she was already dead on her feet.

Tyler put an arm around her shoulder and pulled her closer, then spoke so only she could hear. "No one expects you to keep up with my mother. She's been doing this for decades." Beatrice glanced at him. He seemed genuine and concerned. "Take it easy. Pace yourself. Otherwise you'll collapse in a heap."

Beatrice didn't know what to say. Was her husband truly worried about her? Or was this all for show for his workers? She would probably never know. His arm slid away from her shoulder, and she felt bereft. His warmth was comforting, and she didn't want him to take his arm away, but he needed to finish his lunch, and she was a hindrance to that.

She glanced across at Maisy who nodded, then reached across and patted Beatrice's hand. Maisy was always there, encouraging her, teaching her, and comforting her. What she would do without her, Beatrice had no idea.

Soon, lunch was over, and the men began to take their leave. As they stood to go, there was a knock at the door. Beatrice gasped as Tyler opened the door to the sheriff. For certain, the game was up. It was clear the sheriff knew who she was – a killer. She stepped forward to take whatever was dished out to her.

Tyler stepped back after the men spoke quietly at the door for a short time. "Come in, Sheriff. We've just finished lunch."

"Have you eaten, Sheriff?" Maisy asked as he sat at the table.

"Not yet, but I don't want to be a burden, Maisy."

"Never a burden. Sheriff Walter Ryan, this is Beatrice, Tyler's new bride." Maisy then busied herself filling a bowl with hot soup, and cutting more bread for the sheriff.

"Good to meet you, Mrs. Harris. You can call me Walt. Everyone does."

"Beatrice," she said, extending her hand. She still didn't know if he'd come to arrest her, but there was no recognition when she was introduced.

"This is excellent soup, Maisy. Not that your soup is ever otherwise." He ate a few mouthfuls and took a bite of his buttered bread. Tyler sat opposite, waiting to find out why the sheriff had visited. He'd sent the other men ahead and would catch up with them later.

"I've come to warn you," Walt said as Maisy placed a mug of coffee in front of him. "A few ranchers have lost cattle over the past week. Thought you'd want to know so you can set up a lookout or two."

Beatrice breathed a sigh of relief. He wasn't there for her, and she could breathe easy. For now, at least.

"I appreciate you coming all the way out here to let me know, Walt."

The sheriff stood when he finished his soup. "You sit yourself back down, Walt. Unless you're refusing my apple pie, that is." Maisy laughed, and the men did too.

"No one in their right mind would refuse Maisy Harris's famous apple pie!" He turned to Beatrice then. "Maisy's apple pie is sought after for miles around. At church events, her apple pie is the first dessert to go."

"I can believe that," Beatrice said. "It is quite delicious."

"Well, folks, thank you for lunch. I must be off," Walt said once he'd finished dessert.

Maisy handed him a paper bag. "A little something to see you through, Walt." She winked then, and Walt opened the bag and peaked inside.

"Blueberry muffins. Thank you. I'll savor every mouthful." Moments later, the sheriff was gone.

"He seems nice enough," Beatrice commented.

Maisy stared at her momentarily. "Walt is a good man. It's a different story for those who break the law."

Beatrice stopped herself from gasping. Was the comment aimed directly at her? She's hinted to Maisy she had a secret, so perhaps the other woman had guessed she was wanted by the law? When she glanced her way, Maisy was smiling, so she doubted it.

"Walt and Maisy are a couple," Tyler said.

"We are not!" Maisy objected to her son's words. "We're friends, that's all."

"Whatever you say, Mother." Tyler laughed and pulled Beatrice in for a hug. "They really are," he whispered, then brushed his lips across hers. Beatrice's lips tingled where Tyler's had been, and she longed for more. Without another word, he was gone. There was a hole in her heart that hadn't been there two days ago.

Chapter Five

It had taken several days, but Beatrice fell into a routine. With both Maisy and herself doing the daily chores, she could make a start on her sewing. She promised to make Maisy a new gown once they'd been to town, and she'd chosen suitable material. It was clear her mother-in-law was excited about the prospect.

"You are quite skilled," Maisy said as she watched Beatrice sew the bodice of her new gown. "Perhaps when you've done that, you might make new curtains?" She reached out and fingered the curtains in that room. "These are quite old and far be it for me to criticize, but they are rather drab looking."

Beatrice looked up from her sewing and smiled. "I'm sure we can manage that. I noticed some beautiful material at the mercantile when I was there. It would be perfect for curtains."

Maisy clapped her hands together. "How wonderful," she said excitedly. "Next time Tyler goes to town, we could tag along."

Tag along? "Is there a reason we couldn't go alone – just the two of us?" She could understand Maisy not wanting to go alone, but there seemed no reason the two women couldn't go together.

Maisy seemed surprised at her question. "I suppose we could," she said slowly. "I hadn't thought about it. Oh!" she suddenly said, excitement returning to her demeanor, "we could have a girl's day. Just the two of us. How exciting!"

She sounded like a teenager going on her first date, and it made Beatrice smile. "We could," she said, then went back to the bodice that was close to completion.

Maisy left her alone then. A stew was on the stove for supper. They'd done the washing, cleaned the house, and soon the bread would go in the oven. Although the work here was often hard, and always relentless, she enjoyed living this far out of town. It was tranquil and she could hear herself think. Most of the time Beatrice didn't think about the terrible deed she'd done back in Helena. Although now and then it popped into her mind.

She stared down at her partly created gown. This would be a day dress. Something she could wear on the ranch. The dress she'd worn when she arrived, and was married in, was her best dress. When Beatrice had made it, wearing the gown to her wedding was the farthest thing from her mind. Then again, she had no thought of ever killing another person.

"Beatrice?" A hand touched her shoulder, and it startled her. "Sometimes I wonder where you go, my dear." Maisy chuckled, but Beatrice didn't reciprocate. Her mind went to places she would rather not go, but she couldn't tell Maisy that. "The men will arrive any moment," she said.

Beatrice glanced up at her. "Thank you. I'll pack up here and be along shortly." It would be dark soon, and working by the light of the lantern was difficult. She glanced out the window – the moon was visible in the sky, but it was still daylight. Barely. She'd promised Tyler she wouldn't neglect her other household duties to undertake her sewing, and Beatrice intended to keep her word.

She gasped when she heard the front door slam. Did that mean the men had arrived? And she was still here in what she'd called her sewing room? That would never do. Beatrice put her sewing to one side and placed the cover on the machine. Hurrying to the kitchen, she pushed stray hair back behind her ears. Normally she would tidy herself up before Tyler came home for the day, but today there was no time. She only hoped he wasn't annoyed.

She glanced up as the door slammed again, and there he was. Tyler turned from hanging up his hat and stared across the room at her. The grin on his face warmed her heart. Beatrice couldn't comprehend how she had grown fond of this man after such a short time. What would she do when the law came for her? There was no *if* they came. She was certain the day would come, and when it did, she would be taken away, and likely hanged.

The thought had her heart shattering into a million pieces.

Beatrice lay in bed, unable to sleep. She held tight to Tyler, thinking about the day she would pay for her actions. No one would care it was self-defense. They would only be interested in the fact she'd killed a man.

In the eyes of others, Horace was a good man. He came across that way until he manhandled Beatrice. Of course, he only did that when no one else was around.

She thought by now word would have got out. When Sheriff Ryan came to visit, she was certain it was to arrest her. The relief that he'd come for other reasons was short-lived. Her conscious told her she should turn herself in, but her heart didn't want to leave her newfound family.

Pounding on the front door surprised her. It was the middle of the night. Tyler suddenly jumped out of bed and quickly pulled on his clothes. He hurried out of the bedroom and went to the front door. Beatrice pulled on her robe and followed him.

Earl's worried voice came through the door, and Tyler opened it.

"Looks like rustlers on the south paddock. We're heading out in a few minutes." He turned to leave, but Tyler called him back.

"I'll come with you. Give me a minute."

Her heart pounded. Beatrice knew it was dangerous for them to try to catch the rustlers themselves. On the other hand, Tyler told her they couldn't afford to let those thieves take off with their cattle. If they got away with it once, they'd continue to do it. The fact they'd been alerted was the only reason they'd be checking the numbers, and had staked the area out.

Tyler pulled on his thickest coat and his boots. He was about to leave when he turned back, pulling her close. "It will be alright," he whispered, then kissed her deeply. "I have to go," he said when he finally stepped back. Beatrice felt as though her heart was pulled in two.

Was this how Tyler would feel when she was taken away to be hanged? Tears filled her eyes, but she refused to let him see them. His job was going to be hard enough without having to deal with her emotions.

Instead, she stood in the doorway and waved as he rode away. As she turned back, she noticed Maisy standing in the kitchen, pouring boiling water into two cups. Tea. She could sure use a cup of tea right now.

"They'll be fine," Maisy said in a reassuring voice. Whether the other woman believed her own words was another matter. "Come and sit by the fire." She leaned down and poked at the slow burning logs, throwing more wood on top. It wasn't long before the flames grew higher.

The mere act of the flames growing, and sitting in the dark with Maisy by her side, felt reassuring to Beatrice. The tears that had filled her eyes a short time ago ran down her face and she brushed them away. Hopefully, the darkness covered her weakness, but she wasn't convinced.

Maisy turned to her and smiled. She reached out and patted Beatrice's hand. "We can only pray for the best outcome. Even if they don't catch the rustlers, we want all five men to come home safely." She then bent her head and prayed. Her words were soft, but loud enough for Beatrice to hear. Following suit, she closed her eyes and took in every word.

When the words ended, they both sat there silently. Each was aware of the other woman's pain.

"You should go back to bed," Maisy suddenly said, then stood.

Beatrice stared at her. "I… I don't think I could sleep. I'm far too worried."

She watched the reflection of the flames play around Maisy's face and finally noticed her concerned expression. She stepped forward and hugged her mother-in-law. The two stood like that for what seemed forever. "You're a good person," Maisy said right before she ended their embrace.

Maisy's words didn't ring true. She wasn't a good person. A truly good person would not kill another. She might not have meant to kill Horace, but had she told someone what happened instead of running, he might still be alive. His lifeless body was a vision she would never forget.

The older woman stared at her in the darkness. "I know something is bothering you," she whispered. "Unless it's life threatening, it's better not to tell."

"It's not life threatening," Beatrice whispered. "Not anymore."

Maisy frowned. "I don't know what to tell you. Except perhaps you could talk to the preacher? Or perhaps Walt? Get it off your chest."

Beatrice almost laughed. If she told the sheriff, it would probably be the last thing she ever did. It surprised her they didn't have a wanted poster for her already. The mail was slow out these parts, according to Maisy, so perhaps it just hadn't arrived yet. "Maybe one day," she whispered, and Maisy nodded.

"I'm going back to bed," Maisy announced.

Beatrice stared at her. "You're not worried? I don't think I could sleep."

Maisy chuckled. "I'm an old lady. I tire easily. Besides, we have to be up again in a few hours."

Beatrice shook her head. "I don't think I can sleep. I'll sit here for a bit longer, then I'll go back to bed. If that's fine with you," she said.

Maisy hugged her again. "Of course," she said, and then made her way to bed.

Beatrice sat in front of the fire for what seemed forever. Her head pounded from worrying about Tyler and his men. She would have preferred the rustlers take some of the herd rather than put the men in danger, especially Tyler. Since she'd been here for such a short time, it seemed silly to be worrying about people she barely knew, but she was more than a little concerned.

Besides, a relentless headache that had not left her since Tyler walked out the front door. Her heart was aching, too. Beatrice didn't think such heartache was possible since she'd known her husband for such a short time. Did that mean she was falling in love with him? He was such a kind and gentle man. The complete opposite of Horace. Tyler was more like her father. Sadly, he'd departed the earth many years ago.

It made her wonder if her father was looking down, if Tyler was the man of his choosing? She wanted to believe that was true.

Her eyes drooped, and Beatrice decided to follow Maisy's lead and go back to bed. She might not sleep, but she would be warm. It wouldn't be the same without Tyler lying next to her, but she would do her best to sleep.

Beatrice felt the bed slump and slowly wakened from her slumber. She turned to find Tyler lying next to her. "You're back," she said sleepily. His hand went to her cheek. "You're freezing," she said, fully awake now.

Tyler chuckled. "It's cold out there. We didn't get the rustlers, but we didn't lose any stock either. At least we don't believe we did." He dragged her close against himself, and Tyler's arms went up around her.

"I was worried about you," Beatrice said after a long silence. She wanted to tell her husband how much she loved him, but after such a short time, he might think her a fool. Beatrice was certain he had no such thoughts. In reality, there was no way for her to know. Not unless he said the words out loud, and she doubted that would ever happen. Their marriage was one of convenience for both of them. She needed somewhere to feel safe, and Tyler needed heirs, and someone to take over the cooking and chores from his aging mother.

It really was a situation where neither of them could lose.

She waited for a response from Tyler, but instead, she heard him gently snoring.

Chapter Six

Tyler couldn't believe his luck in snagging a mail-order bride like Beatrice. She was a wonderful cook, witty, friendly to everyone she met, and was basically a breath of fresh air.

She'd been there for a few weeks now, and they were beginning to know each other the way a married couple should. They got on well, but there seemed to be something niggling away at her. Now and then he would catch her woolgathering, or a frown would mar her lovely face.

When he asked if everything was alright, she always said yes, but he wasn't convinced that was true.

"Are you sure you can take the day off to go into town?" Beatrice asked as he finished his coffee. The other men had already left for the day. Earl was the best foreman he'd ever had, and would ensure everything ran smoothly.

Maisy was washing the dishes, and Beatrice faced him as she dried them. The mere act of looking at her set his heart racing, and he wanted to pull her close. Tyler knew he had to control his thoughts. Never did he believe he could fall in love with someone so quickly. When he'd sent away for a mail-order bride, he was convinced they would never have a proper relationship.

His mother told him otherwise. She was certain, given the right circumstances, they could be no different to a couple who had met and fallen in love. She was right. Without that mindset, he wondered if he would have been open to that thought. Mother had always been positive, and without her influence, Tyler knew he would be a different person today.

In fact, it was her persistence about finding himself a bride that finally had him sending for a mail-order bride. Otherwise the thought would never had entered his head.

"I think we're ready," Maisy said, pulling him out of his wayward thoughts. She removed her apron and hung it up. "I want to tidy up first, though." She headed toward the bedroom and it left him alone with Beatrice.

She removed her apron once she'd placed the last of the dried dishes in the cupboard. He drank down the last of his coffee and she took his mug from his hands, then washed it. Tyler pulled her onto his knee as she walked past to ready herself for their trip. Touching her set his heart alight. He kissed her neck, and she giggled. "We don't have time for that," she whispered, then pulled away and hurried to get ready.

"Later," he called after her, and knew he would resume tonight. Having her in his bed every night was not like he'd imagined. The fact there was another person under the bedding helped him to sleep. Holding her close made him feel good. His wife was someone special, and he was lucky to have her.

"We're ready," Maisy said as she stared down at him. Tyler still sat at the table. He hadn't moved after Beatrice left him. "It doesn't look like you are." She pursed her lips, then went outside.

His mother did like to manipulate him at times. Today was one of those moments. She didn't like to be kept waiting. When she was ready, she wanted to leave. Luckily, the horse was hitched to the wagon and ready to go.

They were grocery shopping at the mercantile today. Maisy was choosing fabric for a new gown. Beatrice proved to be an excellent seamstress. The prospect of a new gown, one made especially for her, excited his mother. He'd not seen her so enthusiastic before, except perhaps when Beatrice had arrived.

He reached for his hat and coat and went outside. Beatrice stood with Maisy, and once again, his heart fluttered. He didn't want to admit it before, but

Tyler knew he had fallen in love with his bride. The trouble was, she wasn't in love with him, and probably never would be.

She was well above his class, and if he was honest with himself, wondered why she had accepted him as her husband. It reinforced his belief that something was amiss.

Whether he would ever discover what her secret was, Tyler didn't know. He hoped that one day she would feel comfortable enough with him to disclose whatever it was bothering her.

Unfortunately, he didn't feel he could count on it.

"What are we waiting for?" Maisy said, and Tyler smiled.

"Nothing, Mother. Let's go," he said, lifting first Beatrice, then Maisy up onto the wagon. He placed Beatrice next to him. She made his heart happy, like he never thought possible.

Beatrice and Maisy chatted most of the trip into town. First stop was the mercantile. They had a long list of groceries since they bought enough supplies for a month at a time. When they'd finished their food shopping, the women went up to the back of the store to choose fabric for Maisy.

His wife followed Maisy, who had headed to the haberdashery part of the store. The delight on her face was all he needed. "There's an entire section of paper patterns," he heard her say. According to his mother, it wasn't something you saw often, and was mainly the larger stores that carried them. The two women busied themselves looking at the range of fabric.

"This fabric is beautiful," Maisy said, holding it up against herself. Beatrice studied it.

"It is pretty, but it doesn't suit your coloring. Besides, there's not enough to make a gown. We need at least half a bolt if I'm to make a gown and a matching coat." Beatrice picked up a full bolt of fabric and held it against Maisy. "This one is perfect. I wish you could see what it looks like on you."

"They have a mirror over there," Maisy said, pointing to the corner of the store. "I could see there."

Tyler stood back and listened to their banter. If he didn't know otherwise, he'd swear they were mother and daughter, or even sisters. They got on so well together.

"Why don't you choose fabric for yourself?" Tyler suggested, but Beatrice shook her head.

"I don't need any at the moment. Besides, I'd rather concentrate on Maisy's new gown first." He studied her as she chose lace, cotton, and buttons to use on his mother's new gown. She read the pattern Maisy had chosen to ensure she had everything she needed.

"I thought we could buy fabric for new curtains while we're here," Maisy told Tyler. "This one would be perfect," she said, holding up a bolt of yellow and white gingham.

Beatrice's eyes lit up, and he didn't have the heart to refuse. Not that he would have, anyway. Maisy had told him many a time the curtains needed replacing, and she was right. His wife brightened up his home, but new curtains would add another layer to that.

"Can we?" Beatrice said, coming to his side. "I'd need lace and cotton to match. They won't take long to make either. Window coverings are very basic." She reached for her reticule and opened it. "I still have some money. I'm happy to pay for it." Beatrice glanced up at him, the picture of innocence.

His hand covered hers, then he closed her reticule. "No need. Put it on my account. Anything you want, add to my account." He wandered away from the women then. Something outside caught his eye.

Tyler stood at the window and watched the activity going on outside. The sheriff's office was diagonally across from the mercantile, and he wasn't sure what it was, but there was a lot of activity happening. Four men he'd never seen before headed to the sheriff's office. Walt came outside and greeted them all, then they all went inside.

He scratched his head. "What are you looking at?" Maisy demanded.

Tyler turned to face her. "Not sure. Four men went inside the sheriff's office. Walt seemed to know them." When he glanced across the street again, the five men were heading their way. Each man wore a badge. "Looks like they could be marshals. They're all wearing badges."

He heard Beatrice gasp and turned to face her. She was white as a ghost. Tyler went to her side and put an arm around her. "They're probably here for the cattle rustlers. They're still on the loose."

She nodded and relaxed against him. It confused Tyler, but also reinforced his opinion she was hiding something. What could it be?

He turned as the bell over the door sounded. Walt walked up to Bert, the mercantile owner. The other four men followed, glancing about the store as they entered. "Morning, Bert," Walt said. "Seen any of these varmints?" He handed over a scruffy-looking piece of paper. Tyler assumed it was a wanted posted.

Bert reached for his glasses. "Nope, can't say I have. Maybe Tyler over there might have?" The five men all turned his way. Beatrice moved further back into the store. Her actions bothered him.

"Morning, Walt," Tyler said, stepping toward the group. "What do you have there?" He purposely moved away from his wife, instead moving closer to the front of the store. He reached for the printed paper Walt held in his hands.

The tattered sheets held head shots of four men. He studied each image closely, pointing at one. "This one might have been amongst the rustlers we chased off a week or so back. Hard to tell in the moonlight. Heck, they might all have been there."

"We think this one is the head of the gang. I'll check with Maisy and Beatrice, if you don't mind?" Walt took a step forward.

Tyler's heart pounded. If Beatrice was wanted for whatever reason, he didn't want those marshals anywhere near her. "They were at the cabin the whole time. They won't be any help to you."

Stopping in his tracks, Walt said, "Thanks for your help, Tyler. Appreciated." He smiled Maisy's way, then the group headed out again.

Tyler couldn't believe how relieved he was they were gone. It alerted him to the fact he needed a serious talk with his wife. Sooner rather than later.

Chapter Seven

Beatrice could barely breathe. She was certain those four marshals had come for her. Although why anyone would send so much manpower to collect one woman was beyond her. When Walt handed Tyler those papers, she was convinced the game was up. She still felt lightheaded from the stress of it all.

Tyler didn't look at her even once, so it quickly became apparent the images were not of her. Besides, there were four sheets, not only the one. Her relief was palpable, and now she needed to sit down, but there was nowhere to do so unless she went outside to the wooden bench. Doing that would bring unwanted attention to herself, and that was the last thing she needed right now.

She pretended to be looking for lace and matching cotton for the fabric Maisy had chosen for the windows. "Is a full bolt too much? I'm not sure how much we will need," Maisy said, coming to Beatrice's side. "Oh, my dear girl, you are white as a sheet." Maisy fussed, and that was the last thing she needed. It certainly didn't help keep a low profile. "Bert, we need a chair. Quickly."

Beatrice had managed to get her heart rate under control, but now it sped up again. "I'm fine," she said, waving Maisy's concerns aside. Tyler came running over to see what the commotion was all about, which was exactly what she didn't want.

"Beatrice is pale. I'm concerned she'll faint," Maisy said, much to Beatrice's annoyance. Did the woman think she was pregnant? She'd only been married to Tyler a matter of weeks, so even if she was carrying his child, there would be no symptoms at this point in time. Surely.

He put his arm around her waist to support her. His expression told Beatrice he was quite concerned, but there was something else in his eyes. Was it suspicion? The visit from Walt and the marshals changed everything. She knew it was time to come clean, but would Tyler end their marriage as a result? If he did that, she would have nowhere to go, and no one to turn to. Worse than that, Maisy and Tyler were her family, along with the cowhands she'd come to know.

Everyone at the Mountain High Ranch had treated her with kindness and respect. She'd come to love them all in different ways, and believed they felt the same about her. Maisy was like a mother to her. Tyler... she had fallen hard for him. It was hard to believe after such a short time, but it was the way she genuinely felt.

Bert rushed over with a chair. Tyler guided her to it, making Beatrice feel doubly embarrassed. All this fuss – it was more than she could deal with. Bert's wife Patsy followed soon after with a hot cup of tea. "Sip it," she said. "It will help."

"Perhaps she needs food," Tyler said, squatting down to her level. "How do you feel?" He appeared more concerned now than earlier. And that guarded look had disappeared.

"I'm fine. I don't know what all the fuss is about," Beatrice said, trying not to sigh but failing miserably.

Maisy stood next to her and put a hand on her shoulder. "Perhaps you need something to eat," she said, her motherly side showing. "Why don't we go to the diner for a bite? We can return here later. Bert," she said, turning to the mercantile owner. "We want this entire bolt, plus this lace and other bits Beatrice chose. Put them aside until we return, will you?"

"Don't forget the fabric for your new gown," Beatrice added. "We don't want to lose that either." She groaned then. It was all too much. Right now, she wanted to go home. She felt safe back at the ranch. There were no lawmen running around showing wanted posters that might carry her image, and no one asking questions. It was just her and

Maisy most of the time, and periodically, the men were there.

With everything happening all at once, she now felt faint, but had no intention of telling anyone. She knew it was the trauma of the entire situation. What she did about it, she had no idea. She only hoped Tyler hadn't realized she was hiding the truth. The last thing she wanted to do was hurt these two people. They were her only family, and she loved them dearly.

Tyler reached out and caressed her cheek. "Beatrice," he whispered. "Tell me what's wrong?" She hadn't realized she was crying until he wiped at her tears.

It was all too much, not only for her, but for those standing around her. As she glanced at the four people studying her, everything seemed worse. She shook her head. Beatrice didn't trust herself to utter a word. If she did, she knew she would dissolve into one of those sobbing women she despised. The sort who used tears to get their way. She promised herself she would never be like that, and yet, here she was, on the verge of doing the same thing.

"Perhaps she needs air," Maisy announced. "Everyone give her room." She stared at Bert and Patsy, who suddenly looked guilty, then moved back behind the counter. Without a word, Tyler helped Beatrice to her feet, and led her to the wooden bench that sat outside the mercantile.

"Thank you," he said to the couple as they left the store. Beatrice noticed their fabrics and notions sitting on the side of the counter. At least she could be assured of that. She sat down and felt some relief at being away from prying eyes. These past weeks have been overwhelming, and perhaps it had all suddenly come to a head.

When she fled Helena, she had believed no one would know it was her who had killed Horace. That was borne of panic. Who else were they going to blame? She had been alone with him in the storeroom. They were both working there, and suddenly she was gone from town.

It was obvious who the law would look for, but her traumatized mind didn't see it that way. She took some deep breaths, hoping to calm her addled brain. This was supposed to be a happy day. A day of finding beautiful fabric for Maisy's new gown that Beatrice would fashion for her dear mother-in-law, and also one of happiness.

"I'm sorry," she said quietly. "I've ruined the entire day." Her eyes began to leak again, and she flicked at the tears, almost harming herself in the process. Tyler reached out and grabbed her hands.

"You didn't ruin anything," he said, then leaned in and kissed her cheek. Before she realized what was happening, he'd wrapped her in his arms and held her tight. "You make everything better," he said, then held her tighter still.

Lunch at the diner was wonderful. Her earlier dismay was all but forgotten, and the three sat at the table, happy and smiling. It was as though her distress at the mercantile had never happened. That suited Beatrice fine, but would it play on her mind? Or worse still, would it set Tyler to wondering what was really going on?

If it did, she had to wonder if he would talk to Walt and have him make enquiries about her. That would be the worse thing that could happen. At least from her standpoint. "Beatrice?" Tyler's voice came crashing through her musings. "We're ordering dessert. Are you ready to order?"

She frowned then. How had she missed that conversation? Probably because her mind was still mulling over the morning's events when everyone else had put it behind them. Trouble was, she couldn't put it behind her. If she let her guard down, even for a moment, Beatrice would find herself on the wrong end of a noose.

She glanced down at the dessert menu in her hands. "Custard pie, please," she said, smiling at the waitress, then handed the menu over to her.

While they waited for their dessert, Walt entered the diner with the four marshals. "Ah, Maisy," Walt said, a smile on his face. "Mind if we sit with you?" Adding five extras to their table was impossible, and Walt pushed another table next to theirs. It was obvious to Beatrice he wanted to spend time with Maisy.

Tyler grinned. "We've just ordered dessert, but you're welcome to join us," he said, although the five had already sat down at their larger table.

Walt introduced each of the marshals and explained why they were there. "The rustlers have escalated," he said grimly. "One rancher in the next county tried to stop them, and was shot. Luckily, he is still here to tell the tale."

The women both gasped.

"This makes them far more dangerous," Walt added. "Tyler, make sure you and your men don't confront them. You never know what might happen."

"You're right. It's better to lose some cattle than to lose some men." Tyler was a good boss, and from what she'd seen, he looked out for his men and kept them from harm.

Menus were handed out to the newcomers, and soon afterwards, the desserts arrived for the others. Coffees were distributed, as well as tea for the ladies. The discussion turned to conversation that didn't involve rustlers, and that was an enormous relief for Beatrice. She didn't like talk that centered on guns and anyone being shot. Not that she'd shot Horace – what happened was a complete accident.

If he hadn't… Beatrice closed her eyes, then quickly opened them again. The vision of Horace laying there lifeless in the storeroom sent a shudder through her. She reached for her tea and took a sip. Tyler was watching her closely.

He leaned nearer. "Are you alright?" he whispered.

Was she? At this moment, Beatrice wasn't sure. The thought she was a fugitive played on her mind and wouldn't let her go. She wouldn't be free until she confessed. Her plan was to tell Maisy and Tyler, then Walt. But her conscious was eating away at her.

"I killed a man," she blurted out before she could stop herself.

The room was suddenly silent.

Walt gaped at her, but said not a word.

The marshals studied her – they seemed astounded that she could have done such a thing.

Maisy's jaw dropped, but worst of all, Tyler stared at her in disbelief.

Had she really said the words out loud? Beatrice couldn't believe she'd confessed to murder, but knew it would come out eventually. Right now, later seemed like a far better option.

Chapter Eight

Tyler was stunned beyond belief.

His head was buzzing and his heart was pounding. He knew there was something Beatrice was hiding, but murder? Her disturbing revelation absolutely floored him.

Everyone sitting at their table sat in stunned disbelief as well. You could have heard a pin drop. Then suddenly they all talked at once. Now it was his wife's turn to appear bewildered. Tyler did not know what to do next, so he reached across the table and covered her hand. Her tongue flicked out of her mouth and she licked her lips. He could feel her trembling beneath his hand, and wanted nothing less than to hold her.

Beatrice was a gentle soul. She was kind and caring. He couldn't see her harming anyone unless they'd done something terrible to her. Even then, it would have to be devastating. Perhaps even life threatening.

That's the Beatrice he knew.

Suddenly Walt spoke. "We'll need to discuss this further," he said as his food was placed in front of him. He looked down at it as though the plate contained rusty nails. Tyler surmised he'd lost his appetite, but Walt still tucked in. "You will stay in town for a while? Until we can talk?"

The marshals stared at him despite their food sitting in front of them. Tyler nodded. "Of course," he said once he'd found his voice. "We have things to settle up at the mercantile before we leave for the ranch."

He squeezed Beatrice's hand, and she glanced up at him. A small smile briefly played on her lips, but it was gone as quickly as it had arrived. The waitress arrived to refill his coffee mug, but he was sure it would only serve to churn his stomach further, and declined.

Beatrice leaned in close to him and whispered. "I have to get out of here," she said so only he could hear. He assumed she wanted to leave the diner and not flee Crimson Point. His heart had shattered at her announcement. He couldn't imagine his life without her. How he had lived before, he didn't know.

But that wasn't true. Before Beatrice, he had merely gone through the motions. Got up each day and ate. Went to work and came home. Ate again and went to bed, with the tiresome cycle repeating every day.

The moment Beatrice arrived, his life had changed. He had a reason to get up in the mornings. He couldn't wait to get home at night. Perhaps one day there would be babies, but right now, the only thing that mattered was getting Beatrice out of the situation she found herself in. His brain was going in a million different directions, and he couldn't quiet it.

Tyler couldn't think – this wasn't something he'd dealt with before, and was certain wouldn't ever again.

He shoved his chair back and bid the lawman farewell. It was as though nothing untoward had happened. He clasped his wife's hand and led her outside. Maisy followed behind.

The moment they were outside, he led them away from the diner. Away from prying eyes. The three sat on a wooden bench. He placed Beatrice in the middle. She had comfort on either side of her. Maisy glanced at Tyler, but didn't speak. He reached up and put an arm around Beatrice. She was still shaking.

He pulled her into his arms and held her tight. A tear slid down her face and he wiped it away. "He tried to…" her voice broke then, and Beatrice was unable to finish the sentence.

"Don't say another word," Tyler said, and Maisy nodded her agreement. Somewhere at the back of his mind, Tyler knew the answer lay. He was still in shock, but was certain he would come to his senses.

His eyes scanned the shops on the High Street. It was there he found the solution to their problem.

Tyler stood and took several deep and fortifying breaths. "I'll be back momentarily," he said. "You'll be alright here with Mother." Maisy stared at him curiously.

As he strolled purposely across the road to the lawyer's office, Tyler could feel his mother's eyes burn into his back. The moment she realized what he was up to, she would be relieved. Why he hadn't thought of it earlier, he would never know.

Except he did know. His mind was in complete turmoil. His wife had confessed to murder, and if that statement proved to be true, she would hang.

Emotion threatened to overtake logic once more, but he had to fight it. Had to fight for Beatrice's life. He loved her more than life itself, and he wouldn't stand back and let her suffer the consequences. If Beatrice truly had killed a man, there had to be a very good reason.

He stood outside the lawyer's office, his hand on the door handle. Tyler's heart pounded so loud and so quickly he felt faint. His own emotions were useless to his wife at this point. She was the most important person right now. He had to find a way to save her life. And that's exactly what he would do. If it took every cent he possessed, then so be it.

As he was about to open the door, it opened of its own volition. He suddenly stood face to face with Irvin Madison.

Tyler was no more the wiser when he left the lawyer's office. Under normal circumstances, he would have realized that. With his mind going every which way, he didn't think it through. He did, however, get the man to agree to sit down with Beatrice and decide the best course of action.

"It has to be right now," he told his wife. "You are not to speak to Walt or any of the marshals until you speak to Irvin Madison. Once he has the full story, he will advise where we go from there." Beatrice nodded, but he could see her obvious distress. All he wanted to do was hold her close, but that was not going to help. Not in the least. It might make them both feel better, but that was not practical in this situation.

"Will you come with me?" she asked, her voice barely audible. "Both of you? I don't want to go through it all again later." She took a deep breath then, and let it out slowly.

"Of course," Maisy said, as she held both Beatrice's hands. "That's what family does. Support each other. Especially when times are tough." She pulled Beatrice in for a hug, then they all set off to the lawyer's office across the road.

Tyler could feel eyes on his back and knew they were being watched by the lawman. Walt knew his family well, especially Maisy, and he knew the sheriff would want them to do the best they could for Beatrice.

She stared into his face as he opened the door. "It will be alright," Tyler whispered, but knew that was not necessarily true. Once they had the full story, then they could think about the future and what it held for Beatrice.

"Irvin, this is my wife, Beatrice. You know my mother, Maisy?"

"Maisy," he said as he nodded. "We have met before. I'm sorry to meet under such circumstances, Mrs. Harris," he said. "Please, everyone, sit down and make yourselves comfortable."

"Please call me Beatrice," she said, then sat in the closest seat to the lawyer's desk.

"Now we're all settled, tell me the entire story, Beatrice." His notepad was open on a clean sheet, and Irvin scribbled away as Beatrice laid out the entire story for him. As much as he didn't wish anyone dead, Tyler would have killed the man himself for what he'd done to Beatrice.

When she finished speaking, tears dancing on her lashes, Irvin placed his pencil across the notepad. His hands sat on top of the notepad, and he stared at

Beatrice. The few seconds the room was silent felt like hours. "That is self-defense," he said firmly.

"So she won't ha... hang?" Tyler had trouble getting the words out. He couldn't bear the thought of a rope around his beautiful wife's neck.

"Certainly not! No one can blame Beatrice for what happened. She was merely defending herself. Who knows what might have happened if she hadn't pushed the brute away?" The lawyer appeared truly affronted, and that's exactly what they needed in this case. "Here's what will happen next. We will go to the Sheriff's Office. As your representative, I will speak for you. Beatrice," he said, facing her directly. "You will not speak unless I say you can. Do you understand?"

When Tyler glanced at her, Beatrice was visibly trembling. He reached across and held her hands. "I understand," she said, her voice almost breaking.

Irvin stood then. "It will be alright. The sheriff will need to confirm a few things, and that will take several days. In the meantime, try not to worry."

Maisy laughed a cold, harsh laugh. "You have got to be kidding. How can we not worry?"

"Of course, this whole situation is distressing," the lawyer said. "I need time to sort it out, and so does Walt. Now, Beatrice," he said, coming out from around his desk. "You come with me. Maisy and

Tyler, you can wait here or go for a stroll. This shouldn't take long."

Tyler opened his mouth to speak, but knew it was futile. He was paying the lawyer to do what he did best and needed to do whatever Irvin said.

He watched as his wife walked across the street toward the sheriff's office. It took all his effort not to break down. For Beatrice's sake, he had to be strong.

Tyler knew that wouldn't be easy.

Chapter Nine

Beatrice sat across from Walt, Irvin sitting next to her.

She didn't expect to have an audience of marshals as well, and it made her nervous. "No offense to anyone, but this has nothing to do with the marshals. I am respectfully asking for them to leave." Irvin's words were firm, and Beatrice was certain no one would be offended.

She was relieved Tyler had secured Irvin's services. She didn't know where she'd be right now otherwise. Perhaps sitting in a jail cell. She shivered at the thought.

The four marshals stood without a word and left the Sheriff's Office. "My client is ready to make a statement," Irvin said.

Walt leaned back in his chair and crossed his arms. He studied Irvin for a long minute, then opened his notepad to a fresh page and readied himself to write. "Let's hear it, then," he said as he wrote *Beatrice Harris* at the top of the page.

"It was self-defense," Irvin stated. "There is absolutely no doubt in my mind." He laid out the entire scenario to Walt, almost word for word of what Beatrice had told him. "If this man Horace was manhandling Mrs. Harris, you can bet she wasn't the only one."

Beatrice gasped. The thought had never entered her head. It made her wonder how many other women he'd done the same thing to, and whether she knew those women. She sat in disbelief at the things her lawyer was saying. Everything he told Walt made sense.

"Finally, I am requesting you to follow up on my client's allegations. If they prove to be true, which I'm certain they will, all charges will need to be dropped."

"I haven't charged her yet," Walt said with a smile.

"If I know you, Walt, you won't let it go much longer."

Walt grimaced. "I will investigate this immediately and let you know the moment there is news." He turned to Beatrice. "I won't charge you until I hear from the sheriff in Helena. It could take some time."

Beatrice wanted to hug the man, but she'd been warned not to speak unless Irvin said she could, and not do anything that might prejudice her case. Walt was a family friend, but he was also the sheriff. Keeping the two things separate was difficult.

"Thank you," she said quietly. Surely that wouldn't cause any problems?

Her lawyer stood then and offered his hand to the sheriff. "Thank you, Sheriff Ryan. I'll wait to hear from you."

Beatrice stood then too. Her legs were wobbly, and she wasn't sure how she stood unsupported, but left Walt's office without incident. Once she was outside, it was a different story. Her legs no longer held her up, and Beatrice fell in a heap. Irvin reached for her, but Tyler beat him to it. He led her to a wooden bench not far away.

"What is the verdict?" Tyler demanded of the lawyer once he was assured Beatrice wouldn't faint.

"No charges have been laid. Walt will investigate, and then decide how to proceed." Irvin stared down at Beatrice as she sat on the bench. "Your wife is pale. She's likely in shock. Perhaps the doc…"

"I'm fine," Beatrice interjected. "I'm sure a strong cup of tea will help." If only that would fix everything. "Thank you for all your help, Mr. Madison. I don't know what I would have done without you."

He eyed her sternly. "Don't thank me yet. Let's see what eventuates first." He fiddled with his notepad. "I will let you good people go now. The moment I have news, you will be informed." Moments later he was back in his office, no doubt setting up a file for what promised to be a long drawn out case. Beatrice couldn't bear the thought of it.

If only she'd gone straight to the sheriff when she'd killed Horace. But if she had, she would never have met Tyler, wouldn't know Maisy either. Except for the fact she killed a man, Beatrice wouldn't change a thing in her life now.

The drive home was in silence. Beatrice sat sandwiched between Tyler and Maisy, and felt comforted by the two. On more than one occasion, she'd attempted to speak, to justify her actions, but the words wouldn't come. Instead of reprimanding her, as Beatrice had expected, Tyler put his arm around her. Maisy patted her hand.

These were her people. Her true family. They loved and supported her, and those feelings were reciprocated in volume.

When they'd set out for Crimson Point this morning, little did Beatrice know her life would be irreparably changed. She had no intention of telling anyone her secret. At least not today. With guilt eating away at her, it was bound to come out eventually, and with four lawmen sitting around the table, the words found their own way of escaping.

If she was truly honest with herself, it was a blessed relief. Beatrice couldn't live with herself any longer, knowing she had caused the death of another person. Praying hadn't helped to ease her burden, either. Under normal circumstances, talking to the Lord lifted a weight from her shoulders, but not owning up to her actions was a different scenario.

Horace might have been a terrible person, a scoundrel who cared little about the women he interacted with, but he was still entitled to live. Yes, it was his actions that caused his death, but his death was by her hand. There was never an excuse for that.

"We must put our faith in Irvin," Maisy said quietly. "And the Lord. Everything will turn out for the best." She squeezed Beatrice's hand. It was comforting, and very much appreciated. If their positions were reversed, Beatrice had no doubt whatsoever she would support Maisy equally as much.

They arrived at the archway at the Mountain High Ranch, and she had never felt so relieved. The ranch had become her solace, her refuge. What she would have done without it right now, Beatrice didn't know. "Not long now," Tyler said, and he turned to her and smiled. "Mother is right. We need to have faith." Of all the times her husband had smiled at her, this was the most disingenuous of them all. He might put on a good front, but Tyler was just as worried as she was.

Her hands went to her neck. Would she hang? Because of a man who couldn't keep his hands to himself? The injustice of it all was heartbreaking. Now that Beatrice had finally found a man she loved with all her heart, and a family where she fit perfectly, she was about to lose it all. She swallowed back her emotion as they pulled up outside the ranch house.

Tyler climbed down from the wagon and lifted her down. Beatrice stared down into his face, studying it carefully. How many more times would she be able to do this? To see his handsome face? They should have decades more together, but because of that awful man, her life was about to slip from between her fingers. Beatrice always knew life was fragile, that things could change in a heartbeat. Look at what happened to her mother.

That last thought sent tears cascading down her cheeks. Tyler brought her to the ground and pulled her close. His strong arms wrapped around her and held her tight. "No matter what happens," he whispered, "I love you dearly. I should have told you before this." His voice broke on the last words. "I thought there was time. Believed we would grow old together."

His words had her sobbing. "I love you too," she said between sobs. "I wanted to tell you, but didn't think you loved me." She rested her head against his chest, and would happily stay that way forever. Unfortunately, forever was not within her reach.

That night, as Beatrice lay in bed, she felt stiff as a board. She couldn't get comfortable, and sleep eluded her. There was a chill in the air, and Tyler lit the fire in their bedroom. It was a welcomed relief and somewhat comforting. He'd not questioned her about her revelations of the day, and neither had he accused her. Instead, he supported and loved her. It was more than Beatrice could ask for.

He pulled her close and held her tightly. His muscles were also tense. Not that she could blame him. When word got out his wife was a murderer, Tyler would be ridiculed. Perhaps even ostracized by the townsfolk. Once she was hanged, things would get even worse for him.

Tyler's life would be changed forever.

As for Maisy, her relationship with Walt would be forever damaged. How could an upstanding man, a lawman no less, allow himself to socialize with a woman related to a murderer? Beatrice needed to distance herself from these people. To put herself out of their lives before her actions affected them gravely.

"I want a divorce," she blurted out. Tyler's arms around her went stiff, then he pulled her a little closer. She tried to pull away.

"What?" His voice told her he was shocked at her words.

"I want a divorce," she said again, only this time her voice wasn't so steady.

Tyler didn't speak for a minute, and Beatrice could imagine his mind ticking over. Processing all the possibilities. He rolled her over, forcing Beatrice to face him. "I know what you're doing, and it will not happen. I love you, and this situation only strengthens my love for you. Not the other way around."

Tears filled her eyes. "I won't sully your reputation, or Maisy's. I know that will be the case."

Tyler wiped her tears away. "You did nothing wrong. It's going to be a difficult time waiting to hear, but we need to let Walt and Irvin do their jobs. I have no doubt your name will be cleared." He leaned in and kissed her, gently at first, then more passionately. He left Beatrice in no doubt how deep his love really was.

Chapter Ten

It had been a difficult time for everyone concerned, but word finally came a few weeks after Beatrice's outrageous admission.

Horace Thatcher had ruined Beatrice's life and had sent Tyler's life into turmoil. He did not know if he would lose his wife, or would have her to love for the rest of his days. As he sat in his study trying to do paperwork for the ranch, his heart pounded. His concentration was shot – figures danced across the page and became one big blur. How could he be expected to run a ranch when the love of his life may hang?

He jumped up at the knock on the door.

"Walt! Come in, come in," he heard his mother say. "I've just made coffee."

Beatrice was sewing. There was little else she had an interest in these days, and was simply going through the motions. Of course, she helped Maisy with the cooking and other chores, but she was no longer the bright and bubbly woman he'd married.

Tyler hurried out to the kitchen. "Walt," he said, as he shook the other man's hand. "Sit down. I'll get

Beatrice." It was then he noticed Irvin was there, too. Tyler's heart pounded even quicker than it had before. Did this mean they had news? He couldn't tell if it was good news or bad, but neither man appeared happy. He greeted the lawyer and hurried down the hallway. But instead of sewing, she sat rigid at her sewing machine. How long she'd been sitting there like that, he had no idea. "Beatrice," he said quietly, not wanting to startle her. She turned to face him, but didn't speak. "Walt and Irvin are here." He reached out and helped her from the chair. He worried at her thinness. Her appetite had diminished of late, and he couldn't say he blamed her. He didn't feel like eating much either, but his wife was now gaunt and weak, and it worried him.

They trudged down the hallway toward the kitchen. Tyler helped her into a chair, then sat down next to her. Maisy placed a cup of tea in front of Beatrice. She picked it up and took a sip, then stared at the two men.

Instead of waiting to hear what they had to say, she suddenly jumped up and ran outside. Maisy quickly followed her before Tyler had a chance to react. There was no denying the sound. Beatrice was heaving. No doubt from the stress of the situation. When they returned a few minutes later, his wife was pale. Far more pale than she'd been before. He reached across and covered her hand. "Are you feeling better?" he asked. She nodded, but didn't say a word.

Irvin cleared his throat, trying to gain their attention. "We have news," he said firmly. As if it wasn't beating hard enough before, Tyler felt his heart rate pick up pace yet again. Irvin fiddled with some papers he'd sat in front of himself. "First of all," he said. "Horace Thatcher is alive and well."

Tyler sat in disbelief. "He's alive?" He turned to Beatrice. Instead of her face being filled with relief, she appeared even more pale than before. She seemed to sway in her chair, and he was almost certain she would faint. He glanced across at Maisy. They got to either side of Beatrice and steadied her.

"Take a sip of tea," Maisy instructed, and Beatrice complied. Suddenly, she was on her feet again and running outside.

Tyler stared at his mother. What was going on? His wife should be ecstatic at the news, and yet, here she was, her stomach churning and emptying every bit of food she'd eaten today already. Admittedly, that wasn't much.

This time, Tyler followed her outside. He rubbed her back as she continued to heave. "I'm sorry," she whispered. "I don't know what's come over me." She stared at him then, and Tyler noticed how truly awful she appeared.

"I'm sure it is all of this. It's not easy for me, so I can only imagine how difficult it's been for you."

He reached for her hands. "If you feel up to it, we should go back inside and hear them out."

"Of course," Beatrice said, some color coming back into her cheeks. "I do feel a little better."

They walked hand-in-hand back into the house and sat down.

"As I was saying," Irvin said, with no sign of impatience. "Horace Thatcher is alive and well. You knocked him out cold. You didn't kill him." Irvin smiled then. "He's sitting in a jail cell in Helena as we speak."

"He's in jail?" Beatrice's voice was almost a screech. She was obviously shocked at the revelation.

Tyler clutched her hand. "What happens now?" he asked.

"He attacked another woman, but this time, there was a witness," Walt said. "A thorough investigation has been carried out. Thatcher has attacked no less than ten women, including Beatrice, but we suspect it's far more."

"You won't be charged, Beatrice," Irvin said. "As I have always maintained, this was self-defense." He slammed his notebook closed and placed his paperwork inside the satchel he carried.

Tears ran down Beatrice's face, and her hands shook.

Walt spoke then. "They have charged him with several counts of assault. You had a lucky escape." He stared at Tyler then. Both men knew Beatrice would need special attention for quite some time to get her back to her old self. "I need you to make a report against him. It will help our case against him."

"Of course," Beatrice said. "I can't believe he's alive." She shook her head. "I didn't kill him," she said in disbelief, the relief clear on her face.

"You most definitely didn't," Walt said, then finally drank his coffee.

Irvin stood then. "It's so peaceful out here," he said. "But I have things to do, and must go." He headed toward the door, and Tyler walked with him.

As they arrived at the door, Tyler could see Walt's horse and a buggy. No wonder Walt wasn't in a hurry to leave. "Thank you for everything, Irvin. We can finally get on with our lives."

Irvin studied him. "You can, but I suggest you get Beatrice to a doctor. She appears very unwell. I doubt it's stress. I've seen others go through something similar and not go downhill like this."

Tyler's heart thudded. He'd assumed her condition resulted from the stress. "I will, I promise. Thank you again. I'll expect your account soon."

The two men shook hands, and Irvin was quickly on his way. When Tyler returned to the kitchen, Walt was questioning Beatrice. "I'm sorry you have to go through this again," he said gently. "I have all my notes from earlier, but not everything is covered in those. I'll take what I can from there."

Beatrice nodded, and Maisy held his wife's hand. Walt was careful in his questioning and was sympathetic in the way he asked. Twice Maisy scowled at him, and if the situation wasn't so serious, Tyler may have chuckled.

But it was serious, and it was no laughing matter. He felt for Beatrice, but Walt was right – they had to ensure they did everything to keep Horace Thatcher in jail. He also needed to be there for the longest possible time.

Rather than interrupt, he refilled the kettle. Everyone could surely do with another coffee. He knew he could. While he poured water into the kettle, he pondered Irvin's words. He was right, Beatrice was certainly unwell. She'd lost a massive amount of weight and looked ghastly. He would take her to see the doc and have her checked out.

He loved his wife dearly, and it pained him to see her in distress like this. Tyler was convinced she had given up. What could be worse than the possibility of being hanged? He said a silent prayer of thanks to the Lord for clearing his wife's name.

The heavy weight that had pulled them all down was now lifted. He had not believed his wife a murderer from the very moment the words came out of her mouth, and he was proved right. Now he had to get her back to full strength, and help her love life again.

The kettle boiled, and Tyler pulled fresh cups down from the cupboard. Maisy jumped up and rushed over to him. "I'll do that. You sit with Beatrice. She needs you with her," she whispered.

He nodded and took Maisy's place at the table, but said nothing. He didn't want to interrupt Walt's process. Tyler vehemently hoped it was almost over. The distress on his wife's face was difficult to watch.

Walt suddenly stopped writing, then placed the report into the satchel he'd brought with him. "Thank you, Beatrice," Walt said. "I know that couldn't have been easy. This," he said, patting the satchel, "will help put Horace Thatcher away for a long time. Hopefully, the rest of his life." He turned to Tyler then. "Depending on the judge, he might hang."

It wasn't long before the cowhands flowed into the kitchen. Maisy busied herself dishing out food, and

Beatrice set the table. Her expression did not indicate the ordeal she'd been through a short time ago. As each man arrived, she greeted him and smiled.

"I'll be off," Walt said, and headed for the door.

"Stay," Maisy said. "There's plenty of food. There always is."

"If you're sure," he said, putting his hat back on the rack. He took a deep breath then. "It sure does smell good," he added, then headed back to the kitchen.

They all sat around the table and said grace. Tyler also said a silent prayer of thanks for the outcome they'd been appraised of this very day. The relief he felt was palpable, and he knew he'd never again feel so grateful. "Tuck in," he said, then waited for the women to begin eating, just as the other men did.

Beatrice played with her food, taking small mouthfuls now and again. Tyler leaned in and whispered. "Is everything alright? The stew is wonderful."

She turned to face him, and although she still looked tired and pale, some of the worry lines had disappeared from around her eyes. "My stomach is still churning," she whispered. "I'll eat what I can manage."

Irvin was right. Beatrice needed to see a doctor. This was not stress, because if it was, she would be fine now. She was far from that. Right now, she was a shadow of her former self. He hadn't seen her vomiting before. Was this worry over the outcome, or something else entirely? He supposed whatever it was, it wouldn't go away in a matter of minutes. Knowing she was not a killer had to be an immense relief, but her demeanor did not show that to be the case.

"Try some bread," Maisy said, pushing the platter of bread toward her.

Tyler cut a piece for her and buttered it. She took a tentative bite. He could see what was happening. She was afraid to eat in case she began heaving again. It was probably the last thing she wanted to do in front of the other men. She sat for a moment, staring down at her plate. Beatrice was so thin, and she'd lost her zest for life. It pained him to see her that way.

After lunch, they would travel into town, and hope the doc could fit her in today. He didn't want to wait another day. What if it was something serious, and one more day might kill her? He swallowed back the pain the thought caused. It made him wonder if it was already too late.

She took another bite of the bread. Tyler could see the relief on her face that it hadn't upset her stomach again.

"This is good grub," Walt said. "You're the best cook, Maisy."

"She'll make someone a good wife, eh, Walt?" Tyler was teasing, but he saw the color fill his mother's cheeks.

Walt grinned. "That she will."

His attention has been taken from Beatrice momentarily, but she was still nibbling on the bread. It seemed to settle her stomach rather than churning it up. That had to be a good thing. Didn't it? He was sure it did.

She stared down into the bowl of stew. She broke off a small piece of potato with her fork and ate it. Beatrice seemed fine with it and took another small bite. Tyler noticed his mother staring at her. He'd seen that look before. An idea was stirring in her mind. What that idea might be, he didn't know, but once the kitchen was cleared of people, he would endeavor to find out.

He finished his food, despite feeling guilty about it. He could eat, yet Beatrice, who needed to eat more than the rest of them, could barely stomach bread. There was surely something terribly wrong. Fingers crossed, by the end of the day, they should know.

Tyler wasn't sure he could deal with the thought of losing his wife all over again.

Chapter Eleven

Beatrice couldn't believe Tyler was insisting she travel to town and see the doctor. She was feeling unwell. That was true. She was certain it wasn't anything life-threatening, which was what he seemed to suspect.

She had refused to go, and she could see he was on the verge of arguing. Beatrice had never seen Tyler so upset. Except the day she'd confessed to murdering Horace. Which she didn't do, but fully believed she had.

Her concentration was shot to bits. Her mind seemed to wander all over the place these days. Beatrice had put it down to the turmoil in her life. The fact she might face the gallows. Now she knew it wasn't going to happen, she should be fine. Shouldn't she?

Beatrice sighed. Perhaps Tyler was right. At least if she was checked, they would know if she would live to see old age, or whether she was on the verge of death. With the noose no longer a threat, she had a lot of live for, so why didn't she feel better?

"Alright," she said finally. "I'll come with you."

She hadn't realized how upset Tyler really was until that moment. The tautness in his face suddenly dissolved, and a smile played on his lips. "Thank goodness," he said, then pulled her into his arms. It wasn't long before he pushed her away. "You are so thin, Beatrice. You've lost a lot of weight."

He was right; she had. Some of her clothes swam on her now, but in some areas they seemed a little tight, which made no sense. She would have to get Maisy to help her with taking measurements and make herself some new gowns. At least that way people wouldn't say she appeared too thin. She was certain the way her gowns fell were most of the problem.

She stared into Tyler's eyes. Her hand went to his cheek. "I know. It's the worry, I'm sure."

"We're still going to town," he said. "I am certain doc won't be happy either."

"Whatever you say," she said flippantly. It was obvious he wasn't going to let it go. If she didn't go to town, not only would he worry himself into an early grave, he would continue to harass her to go. "I need to freshen up first."

"I'll wait," he said, then headed out the door. Not that he'd said so, but Tyler was likely going to hitch Bessie to the buggy, ready for their trip.

Beatrice hurried to the bathroom and splashed cold water on her face. She quickly washed and fixed her hair. When she felt more presentable, she headed out.

Tyler helped her up onto the buggy, and they waved goodbye to Maisy. She dearly wanted to come too, but there was far too much to be done. Especially without notice.

There were long blocks of silence, but in between, Tyler wanted to talk about the outcome of the investigation regarding Horace. That was the last thing she wanted to discuss and told Tyler so.

"Stop," she suddenly told him. Tyler turned to her, confusion clouding his face. The moment they pulled to a halt, she leaned over the side of the buggy, and emptied her already near-empty stomach.

"I'm glad I could convince you to see the doc today," he said, concern etching his face.

Beatrice wiped her mouth, then turned to him. "I'm certain it's nothing to worry about. The buggy, combined with this bumpy road, is not helping." Could she convince her husband, when she wasn't certain herself? He shook his head, so apparently not.

"We'll wait and see what the doc has to say." He pursed his lips and gave the reins a shake and they were on their way once again.

Beatrice's heart pounded as they pulled up outside the doctor's office. She'd not met the doctor before, and that alone worried her. Would he be a kind man, or would he be gruff? She hoped it would be the former. Her life had not been easy of late, and she didn't need to add to the growing list of things she regretted.

Tyler pulled on the brake and came around to her side of the buggy. "Ready?" he asked, his voice full of compassion. If anyone knew what she'd been through lately, it was her husband.

"Ready as I'll ever be," she said quietly. Beatrice had already guessed at her prognosis, but didn't tell her husband because of the situation she found herself in. Things had changed now, but having it confirmed one way or the other was the best way forward.

Once her feet were firmly on the ground, Tyler pulled her close. "Everything will be alright," he whispered. "And if it's not, I'll be right here by your side." He gently pushed her away and clasped her hand. "Let's go inside." It was obvious he was putting on a front, as he seemed quite concerned. How Beatrice wished she hadn't put him through all this angst.

Tyler stepped up and knocked on the doctor's door. An older woman opened it, and upon seeing Tyler, her face brightened. "Tyler Harris. It's been a long time," she said, a huge smile on her face.

"Mrs. Talbert," he said, returning her smile. "Is Doctor Talbert in. My wife is unwell."

She turned to Beatrice then. "You must be Beatrice. I'm Doris, the doctor's nurse and wife rolled into one." She chuckled then, and Beatrice reached out to shake the woman's hand.

"Please to meet you," Beatrice said. She didn't miss the fact the nurse was sizing her up. Her eyes roamed from Beatrice's head to her toes. Strangely, it didn't fuel her unease.

"Where are my manners?" Doris said. "Come inside. I'll get the doctor." She ushered the pair into a treatment room on the left as they entered the house. Outside that room were three chairs, presumably doubling as a waiting room. Since they were sent straight in, she assumed there were no other patients at this time. "Sit down over there," Doris told her. You can wait outside," she instructed Tyler, but he refused to budge.

Doris sighed. "Have it your way, but the doctor will tell you the same thing."

Beatrice turned to her husband. She knew he was being protective, and she understood his reasons, but more likely than not, the doctor would also tell him to leave.

The door closed behind Doris, then she heard low mutterings. It wasn't long before Doctor Talbert entered the room, closing the door firmly behind him. "Tyler, Mrs. Harris," he said. "What can I do for you?"

Tyler spoke up before Beatrice had a chance. "Doc Talbert, this is Beatrice, my wife. She's lost a lot of weight, and she is constantly vomiting."

The doctor looked her over, much as his wife had done. "How long has this been going on?" he asked.

Tyler explained about the terrible business over Horace Thatcher, then added, "The weight loss has been over a few weeks, the vomiting only today." Tyler was firm in his assessment. But Beatrice knew better.

"The vomiting has been happening for a couple of weeks now," Beatrice said decisively.

Tyler stared at her, open-mouthed. "Weeks? Why…"

The doctor interrupted him. "You may leave the room now, Tyler. I need to examine your wife."

Her husband appeared stunned, but did as he was told. The moment the door closed behind him, the doctor questioned her. Could she be pregnant? Had her monthlies stopped? What time of day did she vomit, and the questions went on. He leaned down and pulled out some wooden steps. "You climb up here," he said, "while I fetch my nurse." He left the room and soon returned with Doris. Beatrice hoped this turn of events didn't worry Tyler, who was sitting outside the room.

Doctor Talbert helped her to lie down. "I need to do a proper examination," he said. "I believe you may be pregnant." That was her assessment too, but she didn't say so. Doris held her hand as the examination took place, doing little more. She was certain the woman's presence was for propriety than for any other reason.

When the examination was over, he helped her down from the examination bed. "Do you mind if I call your husband in now?"

"That's fine with me," Beatrice said, but wondered at the result. Perhaps it was easier for the doctor to tell them together what was wrong with her.

"You may join us now," Doris said, opening the door to the surgery. Tyler was there in no time.

He stood by his wife's side and held her hand as she sat where she was placed earlier. "What is wrong with her, doc? Do you know?"

Doc Talbert chucked. "There is nothing wrong with your wife. She is expecting. The vomiting should subside in a week or two. Instead of hustling her out of bed early in the morning, a cup of black tea in bed, and a slice of toast, or even a cracker or two, should settle her stomach."

Warmth filled Beatrice. *A baby!* All these weeks she had feared that was the case. Her baby would have been motherless had she hanged. But now, with those shackles removed, it was a joyous occasion.

"That's wonderful," Tyler said with joy in his voice. Beatrice smiled up at him. He seemed genuinely happy about the prospect.

"Your baby is due in about seven and a half months. Maybe a little less. It's difficult to be accurate at this point. Your wife is very fragile, so I need to keep a close eye on her." He pierced Tyler with his gaze. "Bring her back in three weeks. We must ensure everything is going well."

"Of course, Doc," Tyler said, and Beatrice knew he would keep his promise. He reached out and shook the doctor's hand, then he helped Beatrice to her feet.

They left the surgery without another word spoken between them. The moment they were outside, Tyler pulled her close against himself, and hugged her. "This is wonderful news," he said. "Why didn't you tell me you were ill earlier?" His tone was admonishing – he sounded concerned more than anything.

"I didn't want to worry you any more than you were already." It was true. One of them worrying was bad enough.

He shook his head then. "I can't work out how I didn't know."

"I always get up a little earlier than you. Besides, you're weren't always there when I was ill." It was true, and Tyler would know it was.

"Let's go to the mercantile. We'll get you some maternity gowns."

"I'd rather buy fabric and make my own." She would much rather make gowns. They would fit better, and she could leave room to grow.

"That's settled then," Tyler said, and helped her into the buggy. Soon they were headed toward the mercantile. Beatrice hoped they had suitable fabrics in stock. Otherwise, she would have to order some in.

The doc's office was on the outskirts of town, but it didn't take long to arrive at the mercantile. Tyler surmised she would need at least three gowns suitable for her pregnancy. Thankfully, they had several bolts of fabric that would work. She preferred cotton for her gowns, as the fabric was so versatile, and easier to launder than many other fabrics on the market. Silk was definitely one to keep away from. Not only was it expensive, it was difficult to sew, and it often appeared wrinkled, even before being worn.

She chose three distinct patterns, and Tyler carried the three bolts to the front counter. Beatrice rarely used paper patterns, but the mercantile had one for maternity clothes, so she snatched that up, as well as matching cottons, lace, and other haberdashery, to put finishing touches on the gowns.

She purchased enough material to make matching bonnets as well.

"You should start your own dressmaking business," Patsy told her, as Tyler dropped the bolts onto the front counter.

Her husband, Bert, had something to say about that. "I'm sure Beatrice is busy enough as it is, without adding to her chores."

Beatrice handed over the rest of her purchases, and Patsy squealed. "Congratulations," she said, her voice full of excitement when she saw the paper pattern Beatrice had purchased.

Beatrice's heart sank. She was in a precarious situation with this baby. She'd been incredibly unwell. What if she lost the child? She leaned in. "Please don't tell anyone," she whispered. "I've not been well with the baby. I'd rather not tell people I'm expecting just yet."

Patsy's face changed from joy to sadness. She came around to the other side of the counter. "I'll be praying for you and the baby," she said, then hugged Beatrice. A stray tear ran down her face. The kindness of people in this town was often overwhelming.

Patsy went to Tyler then and hugged him tight. "Make sure you look after them both," she said. "Beatrice needs to rest up. Maisy will know what to do." She patted his back, then pushed away.

She returned to the other side of the counter and wrote down the purchases. Beatrice told her how much fabric she needed from each bolt, and Patsy measured it carefully. "I'll bet Maisy is excited," she said, glancing up to look at Tyler.

Tyler smiled. "She doesn't know yet, but I know she'll be thrilled. You'll likely hear her screaming from here." He chuckled then. "I'm still trying to get my head around it. We only just found out. Doc confirmed it a short while ago."

Bert shook his hand. "Congratulations, my boy. Your secret will be safe with us. Won't it, Patsy?" he said firmly. Beatrice wondered if the store owner's wife had a habit of spreading gossip.

Patsy ran a finger across her mouth as though she were zipping it. "I won't say a word, I promise," she said, then wrapped Beatrice's purchases in brown paper and string.

The moment they'd finished there, Tyler guided her to the diner. "Black tea?" he asked as they arrived.

"I should be fine now," she answered. "Regular tea and a lovely piece of cake will do me nicely."

It was a blessed relief when Beatrice finally got to sit down. She felt as though sitting hailed the end of an ordeal, although it really wasn't that way. It was simply a day of extraordinary events. Both of them life-changing.

She ran a hand across her belly. The baby wasn't well developed yet, but it was still precious. Beatrice would ensure she looked after herself, which would safeguard her baby. She was certain Tyler would also make sure she kept well. An enormous weight must have been lifted from his shoulders, too.

She was still shocked at the result of the investigation, although she probably shouldn't have been. Horace Thatcher was a horrid man – the worst she'd ever met. She didn't want to recall the number of times he'd assaulted her, and knew she'd had a lucky escape. The worst part was not reporting it.

But that was water under the bridge now. For the sake of her family, and her baby, Beatrice knew she had to get it all out of her mind. Put it all in the past.

"I'll have a mug of coffee, and my wife wants tea," Tyler said, bringing her out of the dark thoughts she'd been harboring.

Beatrice glanced up at the waitress and smiled. "Thank you," she said.

"We'd like cake too," Tyler said.

"I can bring you a plate of assorted cakes, if you would like," she said. "It's a perfect size for two."

Tyler grinned then. Beatrice knew he had a sweet tooth – she couldn't keep up with him on the cooking end. "That sounds perfect," he said. "Thank you." The waitress was gone before another word could be spoken.

"How do you feel?" Tyler asked as he slid a hand across the table to cover hers. "You're still a little pale."

Beatrice smiled at him, trying to reassure her husband she was fine. "I'm much better. The mornings are the worst. Apparently, being bounced about in the buggy doesn't help much either."

He winced. She wasn't looking forward to the trip home, but there was nothing they could do to avoid it. Traveling into town was unavoidable, but thankfully, it wasn't something they had to do often.

"That looks delicious," Tyler said as the waitress placed the large plate of sweet treats on the table.

She smiled and him, then left them alone. Each piece was a miniature, and there were two of each type. Beatrice had never seen such a delightful thing in her life. "Go on, you first," he told her.

Her hand reached out to take one, but she hesitated. "I don't know which one to start with," she said as she laughed.

"Then take one of each," Tyler instructed her. It seemed unladylike, but Beatrice complied. The arrangement in front of her was enticing, but she wasn't certain she could eat them all.

Beatrice eyed the place full of cakes, then lifted one to her mouth. Flavor exploded on her tongue, and she heard herself groan. Her husband laughed.

"They have a new cook," he said. "Actually, I've heard he's a chef who trained in Helena. Although I'm not sure why anyone would swap Helena for Crimson Point." The smile then left his face. "I didn't mean... I guess there are always reasons," he said as he shrugged.

"It's alright, Tyler. I know what you mean. The restaurants in Helena are always busy. He probably wanted a quieter life." She glanced about then. "I love it here. It's so peaceful, and the people are friendly. Back home, no one knows who you are, let alone know your name."

"I can't imagine living somewhere like that," Tyler said, as he picked up another treat from his plate.

Beatrice had lived there, and she never wanted to return. With her mother gone, she had no family in Helena, and no ties. Crimson Point was her home now, and she never wanted to leave.

Chapter Twelve

Maisy was delighted at the news, as Tyler knew she would be. "I guessed that was the case," she said. Why she didn't say anything, he would never know. But knowing his mother, she had her reasons.

"Beatrice is in a delicate situation, and the doc says we have to ensure she eats. Tea and toast in the mornings before she gets out of bed."

Maisy smiled broadly, and it confused Tyler. "Do you think I don't know all the tricks?" she asked. "I had you, remember?" Maisy laughed then, and her son joined her.

Warmth filled Tyler. He was going to be a father. But not if he didn't take care of Beatrice. She was in a fragile condition, made more difficult by the recent events surrounding her. Praise the Lord, everything had turned out for the better. He wasn't sure what he would do had he lost his wonderful wife.

His mother suddenly stepped forward and hugged Beatrice. "I'm so happy for you both," she whispered, and a tear leaked from her eye. "I can't wait to meet this little one." She stepped back then.

"Now, here's what's going to happen – Tyler, you will ensure your wife does not get out of bed until she's had a cup of tea and a slice of toast. Then she must lie in bed for a little longer. The rest of her day will be easier."

"Of course, Mother," Tyler said, and he would ensure that was true.

"Your wife is not an invalid, but she needs to rest up. She is far too thin, and we need to get her into top condition in preparation for the birth." Maisy put a hand up then, stopping him from answering. "I know, it's a long way off, but look at her. You could push Beatrice over with a feather the way she is right now. That will never do." She shook her head, then pierced him with her eyes. "She needs to eat right, and she needs to exercise. A walk each day will build up her strength. I'm handing that responsibility over to you, son."

He reached out and put an arm around Beatrice. He could feel her bones, and it broke his heart. How did he not notice how fragile she'd become? The answer was obvious – he was caught up in his own heartbreak over the pending charges to see what it was doing to her. He had become selfish and self-consumed. It was a very poor reflection of his character.

He turned and smiled at his wife. "It will be my pleasure." It was something he would look forward to each day. "After lunch, when her stomach has settled?"

Maisy nodded. "That sounds perfect. Now," she said, turning back to the stove, "I must get back to supper. Those men of yours don't like to wait to be fed." She chuckled then, but Tyler knew she was right.

"I can help," Beatrice said, stepping toward the stove.

"Not today, love," Maisy said. "I have it all in hand. Why don't you have a nap? You look plumb tuckered out."

Tyler glanced into his wife's face. Mother was right. "Come on, I'll get you settled," he said, then lifted Beatrice and carried her into the bedroom.

She was light as a feather, and it truly worried him. These next few months were going to be precarious for both mother and baby. He would ensure they both survived, if it was the last thing he did.

Tyler sat watching her as Beatrice slept. Almost the moment her head hit the pillow, her eyes fluttered closed, and she'd stayed that way for well over an hour.

He felt terrible having to wake her, but as Mother had said, Beatrice needed to build her strength. To achieve that, she had to eat. Hopefully, she could keep it down.

He thought back to their visit with Doc Talbert today. How had he not known she'd been unwell all this time? Beatrice had been good at hiding it, but now it was all out in the open, she wouldn't hide it anymore. *Would she?* He certainly hoped not, but couldn't count on it.

The hardest part was he couldn't stay away from work until the baby was born. Earl was a good foreman, the best he'd ever had, but with one man short, it would be difficult to continue their work at the pace they were used to. In the end, there would be a shortfall of income.

He rubbed his chin. It was a dilemma, and Tyler wasn't sure what to do about it. Mother was good value – he didn't know what he would do without her, but he also didn't want to put more pressure on her. Not that she would mind, he was certain. Having grandchildren had been her wish for far longer than he wanted to recall.

The thought made him smile. This baby would be thoroughly spoiled. He knew it already. And they still had over seven months before it would be born. Now that he knew his wife was expecting, he could see her baby bump. It wasn't big by any means, but it was there. Tyler wanted to reach out and touch it, but he didn't want to startle her.

Instead, he caressed her cheek. Beatrice quietly groaned, then rolled over to face him. "Hello stranger," he whispered. "How do you feel?" She opened her eyes and stretched her arms. She already looked better. There was color in her face too, which was pleasing. "Supper is almost ready."

Her eyes opened wide in astonishment. "I slept that long?" She tried to sit up, but moved far too quickly for Tyler's liking.

"There's no hurry. Take your time." She nodded, but still appeared distressed. "Mother has everything under control." He helped Beatrice to her feet then, and she smiled. He couldn't help himself and reached out a hand and ran it over her belly. "We're going to have a baby!" he said, feeling and sounding incredulous.

"Indeed we are," Beatrice said brightly, "but not for some months. I promise to do my best to keep well and look after our unborn child."

"I know you will." He couldn't ask for anything more.

As they sat at the kitchen table surrounded by Earl, Clyde, Buster, and Duke, Tyler was on the verge of telling them their news. He glanced across at Beatrice. She was doing her best to eat, but pushed her food around her plate. Very little went into her mouth.

His wife was very fragile, and no doubt would be for quite some time. Best guess was a few weeks, which is probably why Doc Talbert wanted to check up on her around that time. He could see Maisy's concern as well.

"Have a biscuit," his mother said, pushing one toward Beatrice. His wife glanced up at her, then took the proffered biscuit.

"Thank you, Maisy," she said. "That sounds delicious." She reached out and buttered it, then took a small bite. Then another. It sounded ridiculous even to him, but Tyler was filled with joy. Beatrice studied him, then took another bite of her meal. It wasn't a lot, but it was progress. Even if she ate half her meal, he would be happy.

The men didn't seem to notice she wasn't eating, which was probably a good thing. Tyler would protect his wife from gossip as much as he could. Not that his workers were prone to it, but she was fragile in both body and mind. It was yet another reason he needed to stay with her for a while.

"Earl," he said, not thinking before he spoke. "Can you hang back after supper? I need to discuss something with you."

"Sure, boss," the foreman said, his brow furrowed. "Whatever you need."

Beatrice studied him. She looked none too pleased with him. How did she know what he was going to talk to Earl about? Surely she hadn't guessed he'd decided to take a few days off to look after her? He shrugged his shoulders. There was nothing more important to him right now than caring for Beatrice and their unborn child. As her husband, he had a responsibility.

He'd shirked that responsibility as they waited for the sheriff to share the outcome of the investigation, and that was on him. He'd let her get into a very poor state, not even realizing what was going on. This time he went into it with his eyes wide open, and he would not allow her health to decline even more.

He stared into her face. Was she trying to read his mind? He leaned close to her and whispered. "I love you," he said. "I can't imagine my life without you."

Her eyes filled with tears, but she blinked them back. Then took another mouthful of food. He could see right through her. She was trying her best to show him how much she was trying. The last thing he wanted was for her to make herself ill by eating more than she physically could. She must have realized that was possible as she pushed her plate away, then took a sip of milk.

Maisy stood and gathered up the soiled plates. Beatrice pushed her chair back to help. "You rest," Maisy said. "I'm fine."

Earl was studying them. Had he guessed something was not right? More than likely he had – the foreman never missed a thing. It was what made him an excellent foreman. He was always on alert and picked up anything that was amiss.

Tyler reached over and held Beatrice's hand. "Are you alright?" he asked, her coloring draining a little.

She shook her head. "I need some fresh air. Can we go outside for a minute?"

"Of course," he said, taking her hands and helping her out of the chair. "We'll be back momentarily," he told the others.

They went to the front door, and Tyler wrapped Beatrice in her favorite shawl. It was cool outside this time of night, and he didn't want her to catch a chill. A cold draft blew through the door as he opened it. He watched as she perked up a little at the cool breeze on her face.

Beatrice sat on one of the chairs on the porch. She was already beginning to look a little better. Perhaps she was feeling overwhelmed? It was one of the few times he didn't want his workers around. Right now, they were going through something that was very personal. It wasn't something he wanted to share, even if he saw them more as friends than workers.

She took slow, deep breaths, then closed her eyes. "It feels better out here. I know it's a little cool, but I feel like I can breathe. It felt… stuffy in there."

He could relate. Tyler wanted to be alone with his wife. Being out here felt good. He was about to tell her when the front door opened.

"Here is your dessert," Maisy said. "Stay out here and eat. No one will worry." Then she was gone. Maisy hadn't waited for them to argue, just disappeared into the house as quickly as she'd arrived.

Beatrice turned to him and smiled. "Your mother is always considerate of others. I often feel as though I've let her down. And you."

"Please don't think that way," he told her. "Circumstances have been against you, almost from the start. Here," he said, handing her one of the bowls. "Eat up. Baby is hungry." He grinned then, still trying to get his head around the fact he would be a father in a matter of months.

Soon afterwards, the front door opened again and the men all filed out. Earl hung back and waited for Tyler to approach him. "Ready when you are, boss," he said. Tyler nodded. He leaned in and told his wife he needed to speak with his foreman.

"I'm getting cold," Beatrice said, then stood, gathering up their soiled plates on her way. Earl held the door open for her, then sat down where Beatrice had previously sat.

"You wanted to talk to me?" Earl faced him, worry etching his features.

"Nothing is wrong. Well, nothing from your perspective, so quit worrying," Tyler said. "This is about Beatrice, but it has to stay between us."

"Whatever you say."

Tyler explained the situation and told Earl he needed to take a few days off, maybe a little longer. "Whatever you need," Earl said. "We will manage without you." He stood. "I'm really sorry. I hope things turn out for the best."

It was time to go to bed, and Tyler stood, too. The men shook hands and parted ways. Tyler knew he had sleepless nights ahead of him, but Beatrice was his concern. He had to nurse her back to full health, otherwise there was little chance of their baby surviving.

Chapter Thirteen

Beatrice couldn't believe another three weeks had passed. Although some days seemed like months. Her life had changed dramatically since arriving at the Mountain High Ranch. Most of her time was good, but these past weeks had been more than a little difficult. Had she known she was carrying Tyler's baby, she would have taken better care of herself. Believing she would be hanged meant she didn't care how bad her health became.

Now, though, everything had changed for the better. Maisy and Tyler worked tirelessly to get her back into the best condition possible. She'd even managed to do some sewing – one of the few things that brought her joy.

Today Tyler was taking Beatrice for her checkup with Doc Talbert. Maisy insisted on coming along the moment she discovered Beatrice planned on buying fabric for baby clothes. Maisy wanted to purchase wool to make the baby a layette. Beatrice knew it would be beautiful and made with love.

She also needed to purchase fabric for herself. With her ever-expanding belly, Beatrice's clothes no longer fit and had become uncomfortable. The two women were more than capable of going by themselves, but Tyler insisted on coming. Beatrice could understand that, since he'd said he wanted to hear for himself what the doctor said.

After breakfast, the pair cleaned up as quickly as they could and made fast work of their chores. They planned to have lunch in town, and Beatrice was looking forward to it. They would visit the doctor's office first, since they were all on edge about the baby's condition, and would later go to the mercantile to choose the fabrics they needed. Not that Beatrice particularly needed a paper pattern, but she'd never made baby clothes, so it would make the design easier if the mercantile carried them. If not, perhaps they would order them in for her.

"Can you teach me to drive?" Beatrice asked her husband moments before they began their trek. Tyler stared at her in astonishment.

"Women don't generally drive wagons." He seemed totally taken aback at her suggestion.

"What if there's an emergency and you're not around?" She didn't take her eyes off him. She hoped by pleading with her eyes, he might concede.

Tyler sighed. "I suppose that is a valid point." He glanced across at Maisy. She knew how to drive, but only learned out of necessity. He guessed that could be what triggered Beatrice to want to learn. "Alright," he said, handing her the reins. "Keep your eyes on the road," he warned. "It only takes a moment of inattention for something to go wrong."

"Of course," she said, already feeling the pressure. Beatrice knew how important it was for her to learn to drive. If she couldn't drive independently, and there was some sort of emergency at the ranch when the two women were alone, how did she get help?

"Grip the reins firmly," Tyler instructed. "The horse, Bessie, in this case, needs to know you are in charge." He leaned across and took the reins momentarily. "Like this," he said, showing Beatrice, then instructing her to try.

She got the nod of approval from Tyler and eventually felt more comfortable driving. They chatted as they headed into town, then suddenly Beatrice felt ill. She quickly pulled to the side of the road. Jumping down off the wagon, she emptied her stomach of breakfast. It didn't take long before she felt far better.

"My goodness," Maisy said, when Beatrice was seated on the wagon again, all the time studying her. "Are you feeling better now?"

"A little. I still feel a bit queasy. I don't know what caused that – I've been so much better lately."

"The rough road and being bounced about by the wagon," Maisy said with confidence.

They stopped twice more before arriving in the town of Crimson Point. Memories flooded her mind – this is where Beatrice first met Tyler. Back then she'd had her doubts about her then husband-to-be. In the time she'd lived on the Mountain High Ranch, not once had Tyler done anything to make her think he was anything but wonderful.

He had been kind to her and those around him. In all the months since she married him, she'd not seen any sign Tyler was anything except what he appeared to be – the kindest man she'd ever met. With Maisy as his mother, Beatrice knew that was the genuine version of Tyler. She praised God for taking her out of a dangerous situation and placing her in the hands of these wonderful people.

Beatrice knew she could never repay them for their kindness.

"Slowly now," Tyler instructed as they pulled up outside the doctor's office. "Pull on the brake, and we're all set." He jumped down off the wagon, then helped her down. He did the same for his mother.

Beatrice braced herself before going inside. She'd tried not to think about it, but what if something was wrong with the baby? If that were the case, it was her fault entirely. She should have realized she was carrying her child, but truly had no idea. At least not in the beginning.

Tyler knocked on the door. Doris Talbert opened it, and the moment she glanced at them, she beamed. "Good morning," she said. "Come on in." She waved Beatrice and Tyler into a small room and ushered Maisy toward the waiting area. "The doctor won't be long," she said, then scurried away, no doubt to find Doc Talbert.

"How are you doing, Beatrice?" the doc asked. "You look far better today than you did a few weeks ago." His smile seemed to approve of her condition.

"I'm a lot better, Doctor. I am concerned about my baby. I pray my poor condition has not compromised her health."

"We'll see. Climb up on the bed and I'll look." This time, he didn't send Tyler out of the room. He felt around her belly, checked her eyes and in her mouth, and also checked her blood pressure. Finally, he helped Beatrice to sit up. Doc Talbert held her hands as she climbed down the wooden steps to the floor.

He gestured for her to sit down again. "I am very pleased to say your baby seems to be in excellent condition. Continue doing whatever it is you're doing, and I'll see you in another three weeks. I want to keep a close eye on you, given your previous condition. We don't want to take any chances."

"Thank you, Doc," Tyler said, emotion filling his voice. He sounded exactly how Beatrice felt – relieved and overwhelmed at the good news.

Once outside the doctor's office, they climbed up onto the wagon again. This time, Tyler took the reins. It was too dangerous to allow her to continue in town, he told her. Truthfully, she would have gladly handed them over. It had been a busy morning, and she was tired.

They soon arrived at the mercantile, and Tyler helped Beatrice down from the wagon, and then turned to help his mother.

"Morning, ladies. Tyler." Walt's voice came out of nowhere. When she glanced across, Walt was helping Maisy down from the wagon. Beatrice couldn't help but smile.

"We've come to choose some fabric. Beatrice is going to make some baby clothes." She raised her eyebrows then.

"Congratulations," Walt said, sounding as excited as they were. "You finally get to hold that grandchild you've been yearning for." He grinned, and Maisy smiled back. Beatrice was certain she'd restrained her excitement, and she couldn't blame her. With the way things have been, it was not a certainty her pregnancy would continue. Now, though, things were different. Doc was happy, and so was she. "Please be careful on the trip home. Those rustlers are still on the run."

"I had hoped they'd been captured by now," Tyler said, scratching his head.

Walt studied him. "Seems they might have moved to another county, but we can never be sure."

Beatrice headed inside the mercantile, Tyler by her side. Maisy hung back, and Beatrice couldn't help but smile when she noticed Walt step forward and give Maisy a brief hug, then hurry away.

Beatrice headed straight for the fabrics and haberdashery. She found several suitable fabrics to create some additional maternity gowns, as well as matching ribbons and lace. Tyler took her chosen bolts of fabric to the front counter and returned to her side. She found some pretty fabric for baby clothes, but didn't want to get too far ahead of herself. She would need a few outfits to see the baby through, but until the birth, did not know if it was a girl or a boy. She chose one design – it was yellow with a sweet pattern on it. "I will make three dresses with this fabric," she announced.

"I will knit several layettes, and that will see baby through for a bit." Maisy said, then hurried over to where the wool was stored, leaving Beatrice to complete her haberdashery choices.

She wandered down to the front counter with her purchases and waited while Patsy wrote everything in the accounting book. "You're glowing today, Beatrice," Patsy told her. "Last time you were here, I was quite concerned. You didn't look at all well."

"She wasn't," Tyler said. "Now, though, she is much better, as you can see."

"I'm so pleased," Patsy said, then went back to itemizing their purchases.

The store owners were still working on Maisy's grocery supply list when they left to have lunch. They would return later and collect them, and then it would be time to leave. As they strolled across the road to the diner, Beatrice recalled the last time they'd dined there. It was the same day she'd blurted out her indiscretion of, to her mind, killing Horace.

She closed her eyes and tried to fight the memories. In the process, she tripped. Thankfully, Tyler was right there to grab her before she fell to the ground. "Steady," he said. Then guided her to the diner's entrance.

As they sat at their table waiting to be served, Beatrice couldn't help but count her blessings. Today, she would make fresh memories in this quaint little diner. Those would be the memories she would cherish. Not those from all those weeks ago when she believed her life was over.

Chapter

Fourteen

Tyler glanced around the sitting room as he sipped his coffee.

His mother was concentrating on her knitting. This would be the third layette she'd made, and this one was almost done. She seemed more content lately than she had been for a very long time.

Beatrice was tired. He could see it in the lines of her face. She had a shawl around her shoulders, and was nodding off. He placed his coffee mug on the side table as quietly as he could, then went to her. Gently touching her shoulder, he spoke. "Why don't you go to bed? You look plumb worn out."

Her eyes opened wide as though she were trying to stay awake. Yet she didn't resist his suggestion. Tyler helped his wife to her feet. It seemed like forever since they found out she was having a baby. All those trips to see the doc had been very worthwhile, and the result was a healthy baby and wife.

Between Beatrice and his mother, the nursery was ready, and the baby had far more clothes than he believed necessary. He smiled at the thought. He didn't care that they'd gone overboard. All that mattered was the pair were happy.

Beatrice could barely stay awake to walk to the bedroom, but he dare not carry her. What if he dropped her? Besides, her swollen belly did not make it easy to lift her.

"You need to get your rest," Maisy told Beatrice. "With the baby due any day now, you must conserve your strength." Maisy stood then, putting her knitting aside. "Only a few more minutes, and that's the last layette finished."

Beatrice sighed. "Thank you, Maisy. And thank you for your help with the smocking on the baby's dresses." Her eyes began to flutter closed again.

Tyler's arm went up around her back. "Come on – time for bed." He led her to their bedroom, where he helped her undress and gently lay her down. Beatrice was asleep the moment her head hit the pillow.

He leaned down and kissed her forehead, then quietly left the room. What he did to deserve such a wonderful wife as Beatrice, he would never know. He thanked the Lord daily for sending her to him.

"Tyler, Tyler, wake up!" He was startled out of sleep, and it took a moment or two to have his wits about him. The sun was rising. He'd slept in. Was that why Beatrice was waking him?

"I think the baby is coming," Beatrice said, then winced. Tyler stared at her in disbelief. They'd waited for this moment for so long, but now it was here. He was frozen with fear. For seven long months, he'd worried he would lose either mother or baby in the process of birthing their child. He could even lose both – it was such a common occurrence, but he didn't want to think about it.

Tyler tried to push it to the back of his mind. Doctor Harry Talbert was a good doctor, and it was rare for him to lose either. But it happened.

A hand snaked up and touched his cheek as he leaned over her. "Tyler? Please get Maisy." She winced again, and he knew he had to move, and fast.

He jumped out of bed, pulled on his robe, then turned back. "I love you," he said, then kissed her lips before moving out of the room.

It wasn't long before he was hurrying back to their bedroom. This time with his mother. "Beatrice, dear, how are you feeling?" Maisy asked, putting her hand to Beatrice's stomach. "Are the pains close?" Beatrice nodded. Presumably another one had hit.

Maisy turned to Tyler. "Get dressed and go for the doctor. Or send one of the men. I don't care which, but get Doc Halbert here as quickly as possible."

Tyler was torn. He didn't want to leave Beatrice, but he wanted to ensure the doctor arrived sooner than later. He snatched up his clothes and headed to the bathroom to dress. That's where he made his decision. Earl was his best choice to fetch the doctor. That way, he could stay here and help in whatever way he could.

Rushing outside, he almost ran into Earl. "Is everything alright?" the foreman asked. "I saw the place was lit up. It worried me." Tyler let out a long sigh, and Earl studied him curiously. "Beatrice is in labor? Want me to get the doc?" He held Tyler by the shoulders and gently shook him. "Pull yourself together. Your wife needs you. I'll saddle up and go get the doc."

Earl was right. He needed to focus. His wife was in labor and depended on him. He rushed back inside and went straight to the bedroom. It was empty. That made him panic.

He almost ran to the kitchen. Maisy was there making tea, of all things. As he glanced about, Beatrice was sitting in a comfortable chair, her shawl around her shoulders, and a blanket on her lap. It wasn't long before Maisy handed her a cup of tea. "Coffee, Tyler? Sit yourself down," she said before he had a chance to answer. "Beatrice felt like a cup of tea, and it's far more comfortable out here." She smiled then, and Tyler took that as a dare. He wasn't foolish enough to disagree with his mother – she was a force to be reckoned with. Besides, she knew far more about birthing babies than he ever would.

"Thank you, Mother," he said, hoping coffee would calm his nerves. "Earl has gone for the doc."

Maisy nodded her approval. "Good. Earl is very reliable. I would trust him with my life."

The reality was, Tyler had put Beatrice's life in his hands. Earl wouldn't let them down. It would take something quite drastic for the foreman not to get the message through. Something like Earl being killed on the way.

Panic struck him. Tyler shook his head. What on earth was he thinking? Why had his thoughts turned morbid? He sipped the coffee Maisy had handed him. He glanced across at Beatrice. She appeared far more calm than he did and sipped her tea slowly. Every now and then she winced, and he knew she was having contractions again.

They seemed to be getting closer. *Did that mean the birth of their baby was imminent?* Doc told him first babies took their time. He prayed that meant nothing would happen until Doc Talbert arrived. That could be as much as two hours, but depended on him being home when Earl arrived. He reached out and covered Beatrice's hand with his own. Instead, she turned to face him. "Don't worry," she said. "We'll be fine. Baby is almost ready to come out now."

Maisy glared at him. It was her way of silently telling him not to worry Beatrice. He knew she was right. The last thing he wanted to do was stress her. She needed a calm demeanor to keep herself and the baby safe.

He tossed back the last of his coffee, then stood. "What can I do? I can't sit around doing nothing."

Maisy studied Beatrice. "Take your wife for a stroll. Not too far away, mind you. Perhaps to the barn and back. Then see how she feels."

His brow furrowed. "Are you sure?" Why would someone about to give birth want to go for a stroll?

"It helps to ease the pains. Go on, off you go." What his Mother said seemed to make sense, and who was he to know otherwise?

He helped Beatrice to her feet, and she pulled the shawl further around her shoulders. "Slowly," Maisy warned. "It's not a race."

They went outside, and Tyler helped his wife down the steps, then they ambled toward the barn. When they arrived there, they turned back. Arriving back at the ranch house, someone had moved the chairs from the porch to the bottom of the steps. He noticed Clyde walking away. Maisy had put him to work – she never missed an opportunity for help.

Helping Beatrice into one of the chairs, he then sat next to her. "How are you feeling?" he asked, feeling rather less concerned now that he'd seen she could walk, even if it was a relatively small distance.

She turned and smiled at him. "A little better." Almost the moment the words were out, she winced again. He already knew Beatrice was resilient, but now it had been proven. She leaned back and closed her eyes, and Tyler covered her with the blanket Maisy had placed there for that very purpose. She slept on and off, between pains. It killed Tyler that he couldn't do anything to help, except keep her warm and as comfortable as possible.

When she awoke the next time, she screamed. "Help me up," she demanded, and he did.

"Do you want to walk?" he asked, unsure if she should.

"I don't know," she said, holding her stomach. "That was the worst one I've had." Despite her words, Beatrice took a few steps forward. "Oh, no!" she said, panic evident in her voice. He was confused until she pointed to the ground.

Her waters had broken.

Tyler didn't think he could take much more. Earl reminded Tyler he'd done this to her. He chuckled, so at least he knew his foreman was joking. He guided them into the barn, where they were far enough away they couldn't hear her screams. Not that it helped much, Tyler still knew his wife was going through hell.

At least when she was screaming, he knew she was still alive. Besides, with Doc Talbert by her side, he felt reassured.

"We need to muck out these stalls," Earl said. "It will keep you distracted. Plus, they need to be done. With all the excitement today, they have been neglected." He stared at Tyler. It was a mixture of pity and curious. He could easily refuse to do such a menial task. That sort of thing was normally relegated to the cowpokes, but today it seemed like a good chore for him to undertake. He reached for a shovel and got to work.

Tyler didn't know how long they've been in that barn, but it seemed like forever. The stalls were spotless, and he was exhausted. Much how Beatrice must be feeling. He wondered if she'd had the baby yet, but if so, surely someone would have searched for him.

He suddenly felt uneasy. "I need to check on Beatrice," he told Earl firmly.

"Of course," the foreman said. "I wondered how long you'd stay distracted." He reached for the shovel, and Tyler almost ran to the house. As he got closer, he couldn't hear a sound. His heart thudded. It meant one of two things – she'd birthed the baby, or she'd not survived her ordeal.

As he ran up the steps, the front door opened. Maisy stood there, beaming. "It's a boy," she said, tears running down her cheeks. "Doc says you can come in now. Beatrice is exhausted, so don't expect her to be bright eyed. She isn't."

A boy! He had a son! He was a father!

Many thoughts ran through his mind. Things he would teach his boy about running a ranch. He would teach him to ride the moment he was big enough. He would… Tyler shook his head. Right now he needed to see Beatrice for himself, to ensure she was truly fine.

He stepped into the bedroom, and she was propped up with pillows, their son at her breast. As his mother had warned, she appeared exhausted, as he was certain she was. "Doc," he whispered. "Thank you for everything." He shook the other man's hand. "I'm indebted to you." Tyler wiped at his eyes. He must have gotten something in them out in the barn.

"You are welcome. You need to look after your wife – she's been through a great deal. She needs to stay in bed for two weeks, no…" He shook his head. "Maisy knows what to do. I'll leave it to her. Now, I must be away." He snapped his doctor's bag closed and headed out.

Tyler went to his wife's side and stared down at his son as he nursed. It was one of the most beautiful sights he'd ever seen. He leaned forward and kissed Beatrice's forehead and studied her face. She needed sleep. "He's beautiful," Tyler said. "Thank you." Tears ran down her face at his words. "I love you so much," he told her.

"I love you, too," she replied. "I'd like to call him Calvin Richard – after both our fathers." She stared at him then, he guessed trying to gauge his reaction.

He smiled. "That's perfect," he said. "He'll likely get called Cal. That's what everyone called my father. Let's agree not to call him Junior."

"Agreed," Beatrice said. The baby suddenly wailed. She lifted him to her shoulder and rubbed his back. Calvin was soon fast asleep. "Can you take him?" she asked. "I don't trust myself to hold him much longer." Tyler took the baby in his arms. He was so small and precious. When he glanced back at Beatrice, she was sound asleep.

He carried Calvin out to the sitting room where his mother and cowpokes waited in anticipation. Maisy reached out her arms. Tears ran down her cheeks again. "My beautiful grandson," she said, planting a gentle kiss on his forehead. She then sat down and cradled the baby close to her chest.

Tyler thought he'd never see the day his mother would get to hold her grandchild. "Mother," he said gently. "We've named him Calvin, after Father." Tears flooded her cheeks once more.

Epilogue

Four years later…

Beatrice sat on the porch watching her eldest son and husband. Calvin enjoyed riding, and according to Tyler, was a natural. Despite that, his father did not allow the boy to ride without supervision.

"Mama," Calvin called to his mother. "I'm riding," he said, as Tyler walked alongside him, ensuring the boy was safe.

Two and a half year old Hunter was itching to get up on a horse like his big brother, and although Tyler felt he was still a little too young, allowed some concession. Earl stood with the boy and held him in the saddle as he slowly walked across the paddock. It was the same method they'd used to get Calvin used to the horses. For each child, they used the most placid horses while this training was going on, but as the boys became bigger and stronger, that would change.

Beatrice couldn't foresee it happening for some years, and she felt relieved. Whether their baby sister Ella followed in her brothers' footsteps remained to be seen.

Maisy sat beside Beatrice and watched her grandsons. She had truly blossomed as a grandmother – it was almost as though she was born to be grandmama to these children. Ella slid down from her mother's knees and ran to Maisy. The smile on Ella's face said it all.

Beatrice sat back in her chair and sighed. All those years ago, when she arrived at the Crimson Point Railway Station, little did she know how her life would turn out. Running from the man who'd turned her life into pure terror had turned out to be a godsend.

Having Tyler as her husband, although she hadn't really had much choice, also turned out for the best. Her mother would have called it fate. Beatrice had to agree.

From the Author

Thank you so much for reading my book – I hope you enjoyed it.

I would greatly appreciate you leaving a review where you purchased, even if it is only a one-liner. It helps to have my books more visible!

About the Author

Multi-published, award-winning and bestselling author Cheryl Wright, former secretary, debt collector, account manager, writing coach, and shopping tour hostess, loves reading.

She writes both historical and contemporary western romance, as well as romantic suspense.

She lives in Melbourne, Australia, and is married with two adult children and has six grandchildren. When she's not writing, she can be found in her craft room making greeting cards.

Links

Website: *http://www.cheryl-wright.com/*

Facebook Reader Group:
https://www.facebook.com/groups/cherylwrightaut hor/

Join My Newsletter:

https://cheryl-wright.com/newsletter/

Printed in the USA
CPSIA information can be obtained
at www.ICGtesting.com
LVHW050545280724
786604LV00002B/284